OPERATION

MEDINA

BY ANNE CROFTON DEARLE

Cover designed by Martin Wall

Introduction

On 30th June 1940 The Channel Islands became the first and only part of the British Isles to be invaded and occupied by Nazi Germany for the duration of World War !! - but what if other islands had been taken over? Islands such as The Isle of Man or The Isle of Wight, for example. The occupation of The Isle of Wight would certainly have caused great alarm because of its proximity to the mainland. There was always the fear that the Isle of Wight would be invaded, particularly after the evacuation of Dunkirk, with Sandown Bay being the most obvious place suitable for a landing. Measures were taken to protect the island, but they were not able to keep the enemy from bombing, and islanders suffered loss of life and damage to property throughout
the war. Let us take a flight of fancy into the realms of *What If*?' and imagine what life would have been like on the Isle of Wight if it had come under German occupation.

The Isle of Wight – 1930s

'Oaktree Farm' named for the ancient oak tree that stood by the gate of the farmyard, was situated just south of the old village of Northwood on the road from Cowes to Newport. Its rich arable fields and large woodlands made it one of the biggest farms in the area.

The farm had been in the Barry family for generations The current owner kept a large herd of dairy cattle, aided by his cowman, Albert Granger and two old farmhands. The only other help he had was given by villagers who joined in with haymaking at the end of the summer. The farmer's wife kept hens, and her eggs were very popular in the village.

Albert lived with his aged mother in a cottage on the southern border of the farm. He was the youngest of four sons and all his brothers were fishermen. Albert always preferred the land to the sea, and even when he was a schoolboy, he used to work on various farms during the school holidays. When he got the job of cowman on Oaktree Farm his widowed mother moved from her home by the sea in Cowes, and came to keep house for her youngest son in his tied cottage.

On a lane leading off the main road there was another cottage belonging to the farm,. 'Little Oaktree Cottage', was rented out to a retired teacher, Harold Johnson, who came from the mainland.

'Oaktree Farmhouse' was a long low building with ivy growing up the walls. The heart of the house was the old stone-paved kitchen with its great cooking range and oak beamed ceiling. Off the kitchen there was a scullery, and beyond that a laundry, that had once been an outhouse, but had since been incorporated into the main house. The front parlour with its Victorian furniture and heavy curtains was only used on special occasions such as Christenings and Funerals. The bedrooms upstairs nestled cosily under the beams of the sloping roof.

Behind the farmhouse there was a large garden which was lovingly tended by the farmer's wife. Near the house she grew a profusion of colourful flowers and at the end of the garden, behind a hedge, she planted a variety of vegetables and herbs. There was also an orchard which yielded a fine crop of apples in the autumn.

Beyond the orchard there were beehives and the family enjoyed the honey gathered from the apiary. In fact the Barry family were largely self-sufficient from their own land.

The two old farmhands lived in cottages in the village with their many children and grandchildren. They had both worked on the Barry farm since they were boys and had no intention of retiring, despite their great age. As long as they kept working well Framer Barry was happy to keep them on, especially after the outbreak of war when all the young men went off to join the army. Albert would probably be the next to go.

The Isle of Wight – June 1940

Late one summer day the Barry family sat round the kitchen table enjoying their evening meal. Living on a farm their meal was rather better than the average. There was a freshly killed chicken from their own range, vegetables from their kitchen garden and baked apples with custard made with milk from their own cows. They counted themselves very lucky to live so well during wartime.

The wireless was on and while they were eating it was time for the evening news. It was not good. They listened in horror to news that Germany had invaded the Channel Islands.

"Oh my God!" exclaimed Ma Berry "the enemy on British territory. That's too close for comfort" She was a homely little woman, plump with a round, rosy face and sparkling blue eyes. Her hair was just beginning to turn grey and she wore it in a bun, neatly tied on the back of her head. She pushed a stray lock of hair back behind her ear as she considered the plight of the Channel Islanders.

"Those poor islanders" moaned Issy, her seventeen year old daughter "how will they manage? Suppose it was us who'd been invaded, what would happen to us?"

Issy was an attractive girl with long, fair hair worn in two plaits that hung down her back. She had not long left school and was enjoying working at a bank in Newport. She looked very young but felt very grown up. She wore a stylish summer dress in a pretty blue gingham pattern, and was proud of her new white sandals, bought with he own earnings from the bank.

Pa Barry was silent, busily munching his supper as he listened to the news. He was usually a jolly man, full of good humour, but the evacuation of Dunkirk had shaken his confidence, and today he looked grave as he considered the consequences of the invasion. He was a farmer with extensive lands on the Isle of Wight. His farm, on the road from Cowes to Newport, had been handed down through the generations and he was proud of his inheritance. The thought that his homeland could be invaded filled him with horror and he felt enormous sympathy for his fellow countrymen in the Channel Islands.

"Dad, do you th…." young Jack began, but was shushed by his father who wanted to hear all the details of the invasion.

"Hmph!" said Jack under his breath. At twelve years old he felt that nobody ever listened to him. He only wanted to know if the Germans were likely to invade the Isle of Wight. He felt nervous at the prospect. He was a typical schoolboy with untidy hair and dirty knees. He just wanted to get on with his life, playing with his friends, enjoying climbing trees, and pinching apples from the neighbour's orchard, which was much more exciting than taking them from the trees in his own family orchard.

Berlin – Late Summer 1941

Adolf Hitler bent over his desk studying a large map of the British Isles. 'Operation Sealion', the German plan to invade Great Britain, was very much on his mind, and he had given considerable thought on the best place from which to launch an invasion. He picked up a pen, dipped it in ink, and drew a big swastika in the middle of the Isle of Wight. This had always been a possible invasion site, but now he had other plans for the island.

"This" he said "is where I will set up my Head Quarters when we invade Great Britain"

The man standing opposite him on the other side of the desk stepped forward to see where the swastika had been placed.

"How long were you based in our Embassy in London?" Hitler asked.

"Just over ten years" replied Kurt von Ginsberg.

"So you must know this place – the Isle of Wight?" asked the Fuhrer.

"Oh yes, I know it well. We spent our family holidays there every summer. It is a beautiful island" Kurt told him.

"Is there a suitable building for me to take over?" Hitler wanted to know.

"There is a palace" was the reply "It was Queen Victoria's holiday home. It is called Osborne House and it is a splendid old building" Kurt remembered.

Kurt stepped forward and pointed out the location of Osborne House on Hitler's map.

The Fuhrer liked what he saw. "That is good" he agreed "It seems to be located within easy reach of the mainland. This place nearby, Cowes, is a port I think?"

Kurt confirmed that it would be easy to sail from Cowes to Southampton.

"So our invasion of Britain could be mounted on Southampton" the Fuhrer stated

Kurt nodded "In your dreams" he thought to himself.

"And what is the name of this river that runs through the island?" Hitler wanted to know.

"It is the River Medina" was the reply.

"Very good" Hitler said nodding his head "We will call the invasion of this island "Operation Medina".

There was a silence while the two men studied the map. Suddenly Hitler clapped his hands "I remember" he chuckled "I once heard that the old Kaiser used to visit the Queen at this great house of Osborne. She was his grandmother, you know.   I believe he loved this island. It will be a very suitable place for me."

The Isle of Wight Spring 1941

The plight of the Channel Islands was long forgotten by the Barry family who had got on with their lives in relatively peaceful conditions. The island had been bombed and the islanders were well aware of the damage being inflicted just across the water in Southampton and Portsmouth. The Solent was heavily mined to protect the mainland from invasion, and there was always the fear that Germany would try to invade the Isle of Wight as a stepping off point for the invasion of the mainland.

The Barry farm was far enough from island towns that might have been enemy targets and the family felt safe in their rural home.

Berlin – Late Summer 1941

Hitler had not forgotten his chat with Kurt, and he particularly remembered that the von Ginsberg family had spent summer holidays on the Isle of Wight. He also recalled that the von Ginsberg children had been to school in London. It occurred to him that they must all speak very good English. He sent for Kurt von Ginsberg again.

"Kurt" he said "your children – how many do you have?"

Kurt felt his stomach churn, what did the Fuhrer want with his children?

"I have three children" he replied "two girls and a boy" (What was coming next?)

"How old are they?" was the next question.

"My son is twenty two, he is training to be a pilot with the Luftwaffe. My daughters are nineteen and twelve years old"

"I expect they all speak very good English" commented Hitler.

Kurt agreed. "They all went to school in London and speak like natives"

"I wish to see your son. What is his name?"

Kurt gulped. What did the Fuhrer want with his son? "Franz" he whispered "His name is Franz"

Hitler did not seem to notice the other man's discomfort. He was excited about the plans that were formulating in his head. "Get Franz here as soon as possible" he ordered

Kurt clicked his heels, saluted and left the room. He was full of dread wondering what was expected of his son.

Franz was hastily sent for and duly appeared before the Fuhrer two days later.

"Ah! Franz" Hitler greeted the young man "Come in and look at this map"

Franz stepped forward and peered at the map of the Isle of Wight on Hitler's desk.

Hitler looked at the young man and thought "Here is a good young German, blonde with blue eyes, tall, good looking and strong, a perfect example of the master race." He looked away and pointed to his map.

"You know where this is?" he asked

"I know it well" Franz replied "we spent many happy holidays on that island"

"Good. That is good" Hitler beamed "and your English – how good is that?"

"I am told I speak like a native" Franz informed the Fuhrer, wondering if that was a crime in the other man's mind.

"Good" Hitler repeated "this is what I want you to do"

Franz listened incredulously as Hitler outlined his plan. Franz was to be taken by submarine to a quiet spot on the south coast of mainland Britain, where he would be rowed ashore under cover of darkness. He was to be issued with a bicycle and he was to ride to Lymington where he was to board the ferry to Yarmouth on the Isle of Wight. There he was to cycle round the south coast of the island looking for a suitable place where an invasion could be made from the sea. It must be as far away from the mainland as possible. He was also to investigate possible landing places for parachute drops. He was instructed to find out what resistance there was likely to be against an invading force.

Franz was to be sent for training and was to be equipped with English clothes. Papers were to be prepared for him naming him as Frank Guinness. His cover story was that he was an RAF pilot on leave. As soon as all was ready he would be taken by submarine to the English coast.

Isle of Wight – Autumn 1941

Armed with a new identity, with forged papers to prove it, and with the necessary permit to cross The Solent to the Isle of Wight from the mainland (also forged) Franz von Ginsberg (alias Frank Guinness) stepped ashore in Yarmouth. He left the ferry among a group of passengers, mainly servicemen returning home on leave. Franz was one of the few civilians aboard the ferry and he got some strange looks. What was a fit young man doing in civvies people obviously wondered. Little did they know!

Franz wheeled his bicycle along the promenade in Yarmouth and then mounted it and pedalled off in the direction of Freshwater Bay. His aim was to inspect the largely uninhabited area on the south coast of the island, situated as far away from the mainland as possible.

In Freshwater Bay he booked into the Albion Hotel, claiming to be an injured RAF officer convalescing on the island. He produced his ration book (forged) and paid in advance for a room saying he planned to stay for three or four nights. His room was on the first floor of the hotel, with a wonderful sea view. He looked out across the bay and remembered, with nostalgia, the many happy hours he had spent swimming in those waves when on holiday with his family before the war. Franz loved England and hated being at war with his favourite country. How had he got so mixed up in this crazy scheme to invade the Isle of Wight? He very much regretted the mission he was embarking on.

During the next few days Franz peddled round the island gathering information. He discovered that there were troops stationed at the Old Needles Battery, but that their numbers had been depleted after the Dunkirk fiasco. He was shocked to find that there were only fifteen soldiers guarding the fort there.

On the second day he pedalled over to Ventnor to have a look at the Ventnor Radar Station. He knew that it had been established on Boniface Down at the beginning of the war and, thanks to Hitler's spies, he had also been informed that it was on a war footing. He was not able to get anywhere near the Station, but was able to pinpoint exactly where it was on the map.

His third mission was to Culver Cliff, near Sandown. He remembered from his childhood holidays on the island that the Culver Down Battery was an ancient one dating from the beginning of the twentieth century. Again, he could not get near but was able to establish that it was operational. He also discovered, from speaking to some locals in the pub, that Sandown was thought to be the most likely place where Germans would mount an invasion.

Franz noted that there were gun batteries at strategic points around the island and that the threat of invasion was being taken very seriously.

On his way back to Freshwater he rode along the coast, admiring the beautiful view. The sky was so blue and the sea was sparkling in the sunlight. He enjoyed his ride and was almost able to forget that there was a war on and that he was a spy in enemy territory.

Thinking of the happy holidays on the Isle of Wight made him think also of his happy childhood in London. He was just ten years old and his sister was seven when his father was posted to the German Embassy in London. His younger sister was born in London shortly after the family arrived there. They all lived in a lovely old house in Kensington and Franz and his sister went to a little preparatory school in the area. Neither of them could speak English but they both made friends who helped them learn the language.

Franz had a special friend called Guy, and the two of them were inseparable. They both moved on together to Westminster School where they made friends with the German Ambassador's son, Rudolf von Ribbentrop.

Guy often came with the family when they spent their summer holidays in the Isle of Wight, and both boys loved the freedom they had on the island. They would take their bicycles and a hearty picnic, and spend many happy days exploring the island.

When they left school they went their separate ways. Guy went to Cambridge, and Franz would love to have joined him there, but his father wanted him to attend a German university. He had just graduated in Law when war broke out and he joined the Luftwaffe. He wondered what had happened to Guy. Had he joined the British forces, and would they one day find themselves fighting on opposite sides. He could not think of Guy as his enemy. Still deep in thought Franz arrived back at his hotel and went up to his room. He had a job to do and he must concentrate on that.

Back in his room he wrote his report for the Fuhrer and then packed his belongings. Later that night he crept out of the hotel unseen, and made his way to the lonely spot along the coast where he was to rendezvous with the submarine that was to take him back to Germany.

As planned the submarine rose out of the water, a small dinghy was launched and Franz was taken on board. As he climbed into the submarine he looked back to the dark outline of the coast behind him. "Sorry" he mouthed, feeling deep regret for what he had just done.

The Invasion – Spring 1942

Franz's information had been evaluated by Hitler and his Generals, and an invasion plan was set. Sandown Bay as a landing site was abandoned as it was too well protected. Under cover of darkness, in a surprise attack, troop ships were to land on the beach at Freshwater Bay. The entrance to the bay was narrow and the ships had to come in and drop their load of troops, then move out quickly to be replaced by the next ships Speed was of the essence and the whole operation was aided by the fact that Freshwater Bay had not been considered as a suitable landing place and, therefore, was not guarded. An advance guard of Storm Troopers would be dispatched to capture the Old Needles Battery, whilst others made their way to Ventnor to deal with the Boniface Down Radar Station.

Meanwhile Paratroopers would land on Culver Down to deal with the gun emplacement there. These Paratroopers would also support the Storm Troopers on the ground on Boniface Down.

When the Island had been secured the main body of Occupation Forces would move in at Sandown.

Thanks to Franz an accurate map of the island, marking all main roads and routes to the various targets, would be issued to all military commanders.

Troop Carriers would land men and vehicles on the island, and Head Quarters would be set up in Newport.

Finally, a massive air raid would be launched across the Solent, attacking the mainland coast late in the evening of 19th April, in order to attract attention away for the Isle of Wight, and drawing British fighter planes away from the invading ships..

The date for the invasion of the Isle of Wight was set for April 20th 1942 – Adolf Hitler's birthday.

Isle of Wight – The evening of 19th April 1942

Harold sat reading by the fire on a cool evening in April. He yawned, put down his book and sat sipping his nightcap as he watched the logs burning brightly in the hearth. Gazing into the flames Harold reminisced about his teaching days in Portsmouth. He had loved his work but was now enjoying stress free days of his retirement.   Harold was a bachelor so had no commitments, he was a tall, well-built man with a round jovial face and the minimum of grey hair arranged sparsely round his shiny bald pate. He was unconcerned about his appearance and his wardrobe consisted of an odd selection of old, well darned pullovers,   threadbare shirts and   baggy corduroy trousers, usually muddy brown in colour.

 An owl hooted in the distance and he thought what a peaceful place the Isle of Wight was. The war seemed a million miles away and he felt untouched by its horrors. He yawned again and decided it was time for bed. He made his way upstairs and opened the door to his bedroom. It was a bright, moonlit night and he did not need to turn his light on.   He went to the window and leaned out inhaling the pleasant night time smells.

As he leaned out of his window he heard the distant roar of engines approaching. "Southampton is in for a bad night" he thought as the planes came nearer flying low across the island on their way to the mainland.

The roar grew louder and Harold saw the dark shapes of the enemy bombers in the sky above. There seemed to be a huge number of planes and Harold worried that this was ominous "Something big must be going on tonight" he thought. Shivering, he closed the window and got ready for bed.

Before he went to sleep he wrote in his diary: *"Sunday, 19*[th] *April 1942 - A large number of enemy aeroplanes flew over tonight. There is going to be a massive bombing raid somewhere. Something unprecedented is going on"*

As he was dropping off to sleep Harold thought he heard gunfire in the distance, but feeling very drowsy, he dismissed it as a dream

The following morning Harold was awoken by a strange noise. It sounded like traffic rumbling along the main road. He sat up and listened, yes it was definitely traffic, heavy vehicles by the sound of it.

He climbed out of bed, pulled on a pair of trousers over his pyjamas, pushed his feet into his shoes, and struggled to get into a sweater. He made his way downstairs and out into the garden. The noise was even louder now. He walked down the lane to the main road and as he approached the turning he saw something over the hedge that caused him to stop in his tracks. "Surely that was a flag with the swastika fluttering over a vehicle" he thought. He hurried on and a shocking sight met his eyes. A long line of military vehicles was winding its way along the road to Cowes and he saw that they were indeed German vehicles.

He watched as the last vehicle passed him then he followed the convoy down the road to the village. People were gathering round an armoured car that was parked outside the church. There were German troops everywhere and an officer with a loudhailer was ordering people to go home and stay indoors.

"This island is now under German occupation" the man shouted "The invasion took place in the early hours of this morning, April 20th, our beloved Fuhrer's birthday"

Somebody nearby jeered and called out an obscenity. The officer turned, looking for the culprit but everybody was just standing there looking stunned. No indication of where the voice had come from.

He took up his loudhailer again and continued to give orders "Stay indoors and wait until we issue instructions"

Slowly and reluctantly the people turned away and made their way home. Harold walked back up the lane to his cottage with a heavy heart. The war was now on his very doorstep.

The following day there was a knock on Harold's door and, rather warily he opened it a crack and peered out. The postman was standing on his doorstep.

"Good morning, George" Harold greeted the man "Whatever is going on?"

George returned the greeting and explained that he had been ordered to go to every home and hand a notice to the householder.

"Who ordered you to do that?" Harold wanted to know.

"The Commandant of the occupying forces" he replied ruefully "we are now under enemy control. All the post offices on the island have been issued with these notices and the postmen have been ordered to deliver them. Just read the notice, it explains everything"

Harold took the paper and watched as George went on his way to the next house.

The notice consisted of a list of orders.
- Everybody on the island must be issued with an identity card which could be obtained from Head Quarters in the old Town Hall in Newport or in centres in Yarmouth and Ryde.
- British currency was no longer legal tender and German tokens will be issued by banks instead of sterling:
- wirelesses are banned and should be handed in at Head Quarters:

- there will be a curfew between the hours of 11.00pm and 5.00am
- Anyone trying to leave the island wll be shot
- (and, most alarming of all,) There will be a register of Jews on living on the island.

Harold read the paper twice, hardly able to believe his eyes. This invasion must have been planned for a long time, the orders had been printed in advance and everything seemed to be in place ready for instant implementation. A dark day for the Isle of Wight.

A nice house on the Carrisbrooke Road

Mr & Mrs Brearley lived in a fine detatched house on the Carrisbrooke Road on the outskirts of Newport. They had bought the house in 1925 when they got married. It was really too big for them but when they bought it they had hoped to fill it with a large family of children, but that had not happened.

However they were quite happy in their large house. Horace Brearley was an artist and he had turned one of the fine, spacious rooms into a studio where he could paint and store is pictures. His wife, Marika, liked to cook and enjoyed having a big kitchen with a fine view of the garden, where she could make wonderful meals. The Brearleys entertained a lot and were well known for their lavish dinner parties.

The Brearley's life was idyllic until war was declared in 1939. Everything cbanged then and they became ourtcasts because Marika was German. Friends deserted them and nobody accepted invitations to their dinner parties anymore. Things got worse in 1940 when the police came early one morning to the house in Carrisbrooke Road and took Marika away.

She was interned on the Isle of Man with other German residents of the UK.

Shortly after that Horace was called up and went to join the army. He put the house up for rent hoping to get a tenant for the duration of the war. Nobody took the house and the 'To Rent' sign remained nailed to the gatepost until one day in 1942, shortly after the invasion, when a German officer, who had been charged with the job of finding billets for the occupation forces, saw the sign on the Carrisbrooke Road. He tore the sign down as he had no intention of renting the property, he simply requisitioned it. The Brearley's house   became   the   home   of   the Commanding Officer on the island, and his staff.

Obest Rauch moved in and felt very comfortable, but was not entirely satisfied with his new quarters. He felt that a man in his position should have a rather grander place to live. The Oberst was very conscious of his status, but was rather embarrassed by his appearance, which he felt was not in keeping with his position in life. He was quite short and was rather fat due to his love of good food and fine wines. He dressed in a smart uniform, tailor made to hide his paunch, and he wore shoes with heels rather too high for a man. His chest was covered with the many medals he had somehow accumulated during his long military career, helped on by his close friendship with Adolf Hitler.

One day when he was out touring the island, he told his driver to stop on the Parade at Cowes so he could get some fresh air. He took his binoculars and walked along the Parade, breathing in the fresh sea air. He stopped and leaned on the parapet, training his binoculars on Southampton, just across the Solent. "So near, but so far" he thought to himself "but one day it will be ours".

Rauch turned his binoculars round surveying the coast along from where he stood. Soon a fine house came into view, It was standing amid trees on the hillside overlooking East Cowes, just across the Medina River. The German stood looking at the house for some time, then he made up his mind. That was the house for him. He would set about requisitioning it for himself and his staff.

The next day he sent for Franz von Ginsberg and ordered him find out all he could about that fine house in East Cowes – "and be quick about it" were his parting words to the young officer.

Freshwater Bay - April 20th 1942

Fred Hopkins, a tall, gangly young man with a shock of unruly auburn hair and twinkling brown eyes, had been in the army for a year. He was training to be a chef when he was called up for active service in 1940. He did his training and then hoped to be sent overseas. He had always wanted to travel.

He was sent overseas but was disappointed to find that the sea was The Solent, and his posting was on the Isle of Wight.

He found himself at the Old Needles Battery early in 1941, and there he remained, guarding the approaches to the mainland. He liked the island and enjoyed the free time he got from his duties. He met a girl called Eileen, and things were going well with her. He wrote home to say that he was 'walking out' with a young lady, and his mother wrote back to say 'that's nice'.

Fred had not been on the Isle of Wight for long when the troops at the Old Needles Battery were considerably diminished. The commanding officer called all the men together and made an announcement, telling them that most of them would be deployed elsewhere. Fred did not want to leave Eileen so was greatly relieved when his name was not called out, and he was to stay on the island.

The forces moved out a few days later and Fred and fourteen other soldiers were all that remained literally 'holding the fort'. There was one Lieutenant, one Sergeant, one Corporal and twelve privates.

"You are a chef, aren't you? The officer asked Fred.

"Yes Sir" he replied "at least I was training to be a chef, but I didn't get to finish my apprenticeship"

"Well, I expect you know more about cooking than the rest of us" the officer commented "so from now on you are in charge of our kitchen"

"Yes Sir" Fred gulped, wondering how much of his culinary skills he could remember.

Fred managed quite well all through March, with very few complaints from his colleagues. Some things got burnt and one or two items were somewhat undercooked, but nobody suffered and all seemed to be well in the kitchen department.

On the evening of April 19th Fred went to bed early. He had been busily baking all day and was feeling rather tired. He was woken from a deep sleep by banging and shouting. Then the door of his barrack room burst open and two German soldiers stormed in brandishing rifles.

"Everybody up" shouted a loud voice with a foreign accent. Slowly the men in the barrack room came to, and shakily staggered out of bed. What was going on?

The soldiers were ordered to get dressed and gather their belongings together. Mumbling sleepily they did as they were told. When they were ready they were hustled out on to the parade ground where the Lieutenant and the Sergeant were waiting for them, both standing with rifles pointing at them.

The officer addressed the men. "The island has been invaded and is now in enemy hands. We are all prisoners of war. There is nothing we can do about it, it is useless to resist so we will all have to follow the instructions of our captors. For the present we are to wait here on the parade ground"

After what seemed an age, standing on the cold parade ground in the dark, a truck approached and pulled in through the gate. Fred recognised it as the truck belonging to a local farmer who often delivered potatoes to the Fort. But it was not the framer driving it tonight, there was a German soldier at the wheel.

The soldiers were ordered to climb up on to the truck and sit on the floor. Then four of the Germans climbed in after them keeping their rifles trained on the British Tommies.

The truck drove off along the Military Road before turning inland towards Newport. By the time they were going through Newport it was light enough to see that there was a German Swastica flying from the Town Hall and there were German troops everywhere, patrolling the streets.

The truck drove on through the town and then pulled in to the Parkhurst Prison yard, where it came to a halt. The prisoners were ordered down off the truck and marched in to the prison. There was no sign of the usual prisoners, but voices could be heard yelling abuse from a distant wing of the prison.

The soldiers were marched in to a holding area and told to wait. Eventually a German officer appeared and the soldiers were questioned. After giving only their names and numbers they were herded into an empty wing of the prison and told to find cells for themselves. They were not locked into their cells but were locked inside the prison, and told that anyone trying to escape would be shot.

Fred and his friend, Bill, found a cell and made themselves as comfortable as possible. They were an unlikely couple. Bill was short and rather stout, with something of a 'beer gut', and a shiny bald pate, but the two had been friends ever since they had been called up on the same day.

"I wonder how long we will be here" said Fred.

Bill shrugged his shoulders "Who knows?" he replied.

Over the next few days other British prisoners of war joined them, coming from captured Forts and Military installations around the island. Some had not been as fortunate as Fred and his colleagues, and there were stories of pitched battles and shootings as the men tried to resist the German invaders. Many men had been killed during these skirmishes.

These prisoners of war were to remain incarcerated in Parkhurst until the Germans finally left the island two years later.

The Isle of Wight – Summer 1942

Jack woke up with a start. It was very dark and he must have been asleep for some time. He lay listening to the silence of the night, then he heard something. He sat up and listened, yes he definitely heard voices. Where were they coming from?

Quietly he got out of bed and padded across to the door. He opened it and peered out on to the landing. All was in darkness, no light coming from under his parents' bedroom door. He went back into his room and found the torch he kept in the drawer by his bed. He pushed his feet into his slippers and pulled on his dressing gown over his pyjamas. Cautiously he made his way out on to the landing and crept quietly down the stairs. He could see a light coming from the partly open kitchen door and that was where the voices were coming from.

He made his way to the kitchen and peeped through the crack in the doorway. He could just make out his mother standing by the range with the kettle in her hand. She was making tea. He could also see the end of the kitchen table, and there was someone sitting there.   It looked like Albert, their farm labourer. Whatever were they doing?

Jack stood by the door listening. He heard his father's voice, "We must be very careful" Pa whispered "The Bosh take a dim view of resistance. There can be vicious reprisals"

"I'm not sure what we can actually do" said another voice, "There are no important railways carrying German armaments that we can blow up. If we blow up the island railway we would only inconvenience the islanders. I don't suppose the Germans would care one little bit. They drive everywhere in their big staff cars anyway."

"And no strategic bridges that we can destroy to impede army movements" added someone else. "Although I suppose we could blow up the floating bridge between East and West Cowes, but that would inconvenience islanders too"

"Nevertheless, we must form some sort of resistance movement" announced Pa, "we can't just sit back and submit. We must be ready to take whatever action we can. Something will turn up"

"I think I might be able to help I some way" came the distinctive voice of Harold, " As you know I was……."

But he was suddenly interrupted as Jack gently pushed the door slightly more open so he could see who else was in the kitchen, but that was a mistake. Albert saw the door move and jumped to his feet "Who's there?" he called nervously.

The next thing Jack knew, the door flung open and he was confronting his father.

"Jack!" exclaimed Pa "Whatever are you doing down here in the middle of the night?"

"I – er – I heard a n-n-noise" Jack stammered "I came to see what it was"

"That was very brave of you" called his mother coming across and putting her arm round him. "Come on in. Would you like some cocoa?"

She propelled him across the kitchen to a stool by the range. Sitting down he looked round the kitchen. To his surprise he saw not only Albert sitting at the kitchen table but also Pete and his son, John, from the neighbouring farm, and Harold who lived in the cottage down the road.

"How long were you standing there" asked Pa "What did you hear?"

"I think I heard something about a resistance movement" Jack told him "Are you going to fight the Germans?"

"It is all very secret" Pa said "You must never tell a soul what you heard. I wish you had not come down"

"Now he knows he should join the group" suggested John "I think he could be very useful. A boy could move around more freely without rousing suspicion."

"Yes" agreed Pete "he could be our messenger boy. The Germans would not take any notice of a boy on his bike."

"No" protested Ma "I don't want him involved. It could be dangerous"

"But I would like to be involved. Please let ….." Jack began but was interrupted by Ma.

"You be quiet" she ordered "I am not having you getting into any danger"

"Now then Ma", Pa joined in the argument "He is already involved. He has heard what we said, he knows what we plan to do. Anyway, I agree with John, we need a messenger boy and Jack would be ideal"

Jack grinned. He was excited to be part of a resistance group. Pity it had to be a secret, it would be a great story to tell his pals at school.

Pa turned back to the group at the table "You were just about to say something, Harold" he said "What did you want to tell us?"

"Ah yes" Harold continued as if he had not been interrupted "As you know I was a language teacher at the Grammar School in Portsmouth. I taught French but personally I also spoke several other languages as well" he paused for effect. The others were watching him intently "Including German" he finished in triumph.

There was no response.

"Well, don't you see" he continued, sounding rather irritated. "I could eaves drop on conversations. There are always a lot of German soldiers in our local pub. They chat away in their own language in the belief that nobody can understand them. I could listen in and find out if there is anything going to happen that could be of use to us"

"Oh yes, I see what you mean" Pa agreed "That could be very handy. We will keep your knowledge of the German language a secret then you can report back to us what you have heard"

There was more general discussion and then the group broke up. Pete and his son went first, followed shortly by Harold. They were all going to make their way home across the fields, carefully avoiding being seen breaking the curfew.

By the time Jack went back to bed his mother had been placated and he had been initiated into the group. He was sworn to secrecy, not even his sister, Issy, was to know about the group. He climbed back into bed and pulled the blanket up round his neck, but it was a long time before he was able to sleep.

He hated to have to keep a secret from his best friend, Freddy. They shared everything and Jack would like to have told him all about the 'Group', but he had promised to tell no-one, so it had to be. It was a pity, really, because Freddy would have been a great ally.

The Isle of Wight - Summer 1942

With the occupation of the Isle of Wight complete Frank Guinness became Franz von Ginsberg once again and was restored to his rank of Leutnant (Pilot Officer) in the Luftwaffe. However he did not return to his duties in Germany. He was, instead, appointed as interpreter and liaison officer on the island. This, he discovered, meant undertaking some very unpleasant duties such as the one he found himself embarking on early one morning in the summer of 1942.

The Commanding Officer of the occupation forces was a bully of a man called Oberst (Colonel) Rauch, a stocky, red-faced individual with a 'bullet' head and a monocle he wore on one eye. He sent for Franz one day and ordered him to requisition a fine house in East Cowes, where he planned to set up his Head Quarters. He had done some research and had discovered that the property was occupied by an elderly widow who lived there alone, except for a small staff. Franz was ordered to turn the old lady out of her home and commandeer it for the Oberst.

So it was that Franz found himself standing on the doorstep of Hill House, waiting for someone to answer the bell. After some time the door was opened by a middle aged man wearing what looked like a chauffeur's uniform.

"What can I do for you?" he asked eyeing the young officer's Luftwaffe uniform.

"I need to speak to the Lady of the house" Franz replied politely.

"My Lady is not receiving visitors today" grunted the other man attempting to shut the door, but Franz had anticipated such a reaction and already had his foot strategically placed to keep the door from closing. The man looked down at Franz's foot and shrugged his shoulders "I suppose you had better come in" he relented.

Franz went in through a small porch and found himself in a large open hall. He was told to wait there. As he waited he looked around. He could see why the Oberst wanted this house, it was magnificent. He was standing in front of a fine marble fireplace. There was no fire burning but there was a basket of pine cones placed artistically in the empty hearth. Behind him he saw a great oak staircase winding its way up to a minstrel's gallery on the floor above. One wall was occupied by a huge bookcase, reaching from the floor to the ceiling. It was full of leather bound volumes in a range of colours, giving the whole room a colourful glow. He was just wondering whether he dared to take a volume down when the servant returned.

Franz was shown into an impressive parlour and confronted by a formidable elderly lady. She was very tall, almost as tall as Franz. She was wearing a soft lilac wool dress that clung to her slim figure and she had a long string of pearls round her neck. Her grey hair was cut quite short and curled round her face in such a way that it made her dark eyes look huge. She turned these eyes on Franz and gave him a penetrating stare.

Lady Worthington-Brown was the widow of a wealthy London banker who had died just before war was declared. She had decided to close up her London home and move to what she thought was the safety of her country house on the Isle of Wight Not the best move, she had since discovered, as she now found herself living in occupied territory.

Franz clicked his heels and saluted "Madam" he began

"Don't you 'madam' me, young man. I am usually addressed as 'My Lady'" he was informed.

Franz gulped "I am here to present you with a requisition order, My Lady" he said, holding out the document to her. She made no move to take it.

"As you do not seem inclined to read the document I will tell you what it says. It informs you that ………"

"You speak remarkably good English" Lady Worthington-Brown interrupted. "Surely you cannot be British"

" No Madam – I mean My Lady" Franz paused from what he was reading. "I am German but was educated in London. May I continue?"

In the absence of a reply he went on to tell her that Oberst Rauch required her to leave her house so that he could set up his HQ there.

The lady was furious "You can tell your Oberst, or whatever he calls himself, that I have no intention of leaving my home and he can go and find somewhere else to live. Good Morning" and she turned and pulled a heavy bell rope hanging by the fireplace.

The chauffeur responded so quickly that Franz was convinced he had been listening outside the door.

"Show this gentleman out, Higgs" Lady Worthington-Brown instructed. Higgs held the door open for Franz, but the young officer made no move to leave.

"Look Madam – I mean My Lady, I hate this and I want to make it as easy as I can for you. You have no choice in the matter. Either you leave of your own free will, or you will be forcibly removed. I would not like to see you undergoing such indignity so I urge you to listen to what I have to say, and to act accordingly"

Lady Worthington-Brown sat down, looking somewhat deflated.

Higgs went and stood beside her "How forcibly?" he asked.

"Soldiers will come and arrest the lady" Franz replied "She will be held on a charge of obstruction She could remain in prison for some time' If, and when she was released she would not be able to return here. Oberst Rauch will take her house whether she likes it or not"

Higgs and his lady looked aghast.

"Suppose Her Ladyship leaves as requested – what will happen then? Higgs wanted to know.

"She will have to find somewhere to live, of course, but she will be left in peace." Franz reassured him.

"May I speak to Her Ladyship alone for a moment" Higgs asked.

Franz agreed and was shown to another room to await the outcome of Higgs' discussion with Lady Worthington-Brown. He felt sure that Oberst Rauch would not approve of the way he was handling the matter. He had been instructed to turn the lady out, not to encourage her to leave peaceably. Franz loved England and hated being at war with people he regarded as his friends. Despite her haughty manner Franz rather liked the feisty old lady, and could not bear to think of her being humiliated. He sincerely hoped that Higgs would make her see reason. Higgs clearly had a better grasp of the situation

Eventually Higgs returned and told Franz that Her ladyship would be leaving first thing the following morning. Franz did not ask how the man had managed to achieve this outcome, but was grateful that it had turned out that way.

"The Oberst will be moving in at lunch time tomorrow" he informed the chauffeur "that should give you time to pack up the lady's personal belongings." He clicked his heels, saluted and left with as much dignity as he could muster.

Franz wondered how the chauffeur had managed to persuade the old lady to change her mind. He could not have imagined how difficult it was. The chauffeur, Higgs, had stood facing his boss to launch into the most difficult speech of his life.

"My Lady" he began "if you refuse to move out the German Secret Police will come and take you away by force. You would be held in prison in terrible conditions, probably until you died. And what would it all be for? The answer is just for your own pride"

The old lady looked horrified and was about to protest, but Higgs pressed on before she could speak.

""If you go of your own free will you will live to see Germany defeated, I am sure of it. Now then, I have a plan. You are probably wondering where you would go if you left your house. This is what I suggest, come and live in the lodge with Doris and me. As you know our son, Arthur, was called up and went to join the army on the mainland just before the island was invaded. So his room is empty at present and will be until the war is won. You can have his room. It is only small, but it is warm and comfortable, and you are welcome to have it. The lodge is yours in any case, so you would still be living in your own property. What do you say?"

Higgs was sweating by this time, he had never been so outspoken with his employer before and wondered if he was going to be sacked on the spot. To his amazement the old lady sat down and a small tear trickled down her cheek.

"Thank you Higgs" she whispered "there is wisdom in your words. I accept your offer very gratefully. But have you spoken to your wife about this? What is she going to think about it?"

Higgs had to admit that Doris, who was her Ladyship's cook, knew nothing of the matter. He had needed to take an instant decision and there had been no time to speak to Doris.

"I will go and tell the Officer that you will be moving out tomorrow and then I will go and talk to Doris" he said and left, with some trepidation, to face his wife.

"You did what?" snapped Doris when he told her what he had done "Are you mad? How can we have Her Ladyship living in our home? And what if Arthur comes home? Where will he go?"

"Doris! Doris! Where is your compassion? Her Ladyship is being turned out of her home, where can she go. And let's face it, the lodge belongs to her anyway. As to Arthur, we both know very well he cannot come home until this dreadful war is over. We live in occupied territory, he cannot just swan in whenever he feels like it"

Doris blushed. She realised that she was being unkind. But having Her Ladyship living at such close quarters was not a prospect she relished "Oh well" she sighed "I suppose it is a done deal. When is she moving in?"

"Tomorrow" Higgs replied as he dodged the wet tea towel that came flying past his ear.

Plans to escape from prison

Fred Hopkins found himself once more in charge of a kitchen. The senior officer of the prison camp in Parkhurst somehow got to hear that Fred was a chef, and he appointed him to take charge of catering for the prisoners of war. Fred agreed on condition he could have his pal, Bill as an assistant.

The Germans supplied the prison with food, albeit somewhat limited, and Fred did his best to make it palatable. Life was very busy for the two soldiers and they had little time for leisure. Sometimes they were able to join their fellow prisoners for a game of football in the exercise yard, and when the weather was warm enough they would take time to sit of the steps of the kitchen and smoke a leisurely cigarette. This was a rare treat as cigarettes were like gold dust and could be used as currency to buy extra food, so Fred and Bill were in a good position to receive the odd bribe.

One day Fred and Bill were busily preparing lunch when Bill suddenly stopped peeling potatoes and declared that he had a brainwave.

"Get on with them spuds" Fred ordered "we don't have time for any silly ideas today"

"It's not a silly idea" Bill declared "it's ...."

"Sh!" Fred warned "someone's coming"

The two men got on with their work as a German guard came into the kitchen and stood by the door watching them

As soon as the soldier had moved away Bill continues with what he had been trying to say. "I have an escape plan" he whispered.

"Don't be daft" Fred scoffed. "How can we escape? Even if we managed to get out of this place where would we go? Have you forgotten that we're on an island?".

"I hadn't got that far yet. I was just thinking of how to get out of here and I have the perfect plan for that"

"Well, it's no good if you can't get off the island. So get on with your work and stop day dreaming"

Bill shrugged his shoulders, gave Fred a dirty look and got on with the potatoes.

Bill could not forget his plan to get out of the prison and the following day he came to the kitchen with another inmate. "This is Jim" he said, introducing his friend.

"How do" Fred greeted the other man as he went on mixing his pastry.

"Jim knows a man on the island. He used to live in Portsmouth and his old French teacher moved to the Isle of Wight when he retired. He would hide us until we could find a boat to get off the island".

"You're not still harping on about that, are you?" was Fred's response. "You can't ask anyone to shelter you. Think of the danger you would be putting that man in".

"We have made up our minds" Bill insisted "we have even spoken to our senior officer, Major Thomkins, and he said we are duty bound to try and escape. So we are going, with or without you"

"I don't want to leave the island" Fred told him "my girl is here and if I leave I may never get back to find her. So I'm staying put"

Then it's just you and me, Bill" stated Jim, speaking for the first time.

Her Ladyship makes a confession

Higgs was sitting upright in his chair looking rather uncomfortable. It did not seem right sitting in the presence of Her Ladyship. He was holding his pipe in his hand, not quite liking to light up.

Dora Higgs was sitting by the fire, knitting. She, too, felt rather uncomfortable in the presence of Her Ladyship.

Her Ladyship, on the other hand, looked very much at ease. She was sitting on the settee gazing thoughtfully into the fire. Suddenly she seemed to make up her mind about whatever had been troubling her. "I have something to tell you" she announced, causing her two companions to turn their attention to her.

"There is something I think you should know" she continued "something that may make our lives more comfortable if we are to live together. The fact is, I am not what I seem to be"

Higgs stared at her in amazement, wondering what was coming next. His wife continued knitting, seemingly unimpressed by Her Ladyship's forthcoming confession.

"I was born in the East End of London" Her Ladyship announced "I expect you thought I was born in some stately home with servants to care for me, but that was not so." She paused to see the reaction to what she had said. Higgs and his wife were now fully focussed on her.

"I grew up in a small terraced house and went to the local council school. I was quite bright and won a scholarship to the Grammar School. The Governors of that school had set up a fund to support bright pupils and enable them to go into further education, so when I left school I went to a secretarial college. This meant I was eventually able to get a good job as a typist in a private bank."

Again she paused. Higgs and his wife waited for her to continue.

"The Chairman of the bank had a son who was to follow in his father's footsteps. He had to start at the bottom and work his way up so that he would understand every aspect of the bank. So he began as office boy, and one of his jobs was to collect the post from the typing pool. One day, I went to the local park to eat my sandwiches for lunch. I was sitting on a park bench enjoying the sunshine when the Chairman's son suddenly appeared and sat down next to me. He told me he had noticed me in the typing pool and would like to get to know me. Well, I was amazed and did not quite know how to react to that. Anyway, to cut a long story short, we did get to know each other very well. Every day we would eat our lunch in the park and at weekends we would go for long bus rides to places like Kew Gardens or Richmond Park, and we would walk together. A few months later, whilst on one of our walks, he proposed to me"

Again Her Ladyship paused. Higgs and his wife were, by this time, mesmerised. "Go on" murmured Dora.

"Needless to say The Chairman and his wife were horrified.   Henry, that was the son's name, was forbidden to have anything more to do with me. They would never permit him to marry a common little typist from the East End.   Shortly after Henry announced that he wanted to marry me I was given the sack from the bank. My work was not up to standard was the reason given"

"No!" exclaimed Dora "That was dreadful"

"Indeed it was" replied Her ladyship. "It meant that I did not get a reference and could not find another job. As it turned out I did not need another job. Henry got a special licence and married me anyway. We were married in the Registry Office at Caxton Hall. My parents were there but nobody from Henry's family. After the ceremony Henry took me to meet his parents. They lived in a grand house in Belgravia, one of the most expensive areas of London. I was terrified and quite justly so. His parents were horrible. They would have nothing to do with me. There was a terrible row and Henry stormed out of the house dragging me after him."

"What happened then?" Higgs wanted to know.

"Henry rented a small flat for us and he continued to work at the bank, but it was not a happy time for him. I got a job in a florist shop round the corner from our flat so I was able to contribute to the household expenses. Eventually Henry worked his way up through the bank and when his father died he became the Chairman. Also he inherited his father's title and became Sir Henry Worthington-Brown Bt. I was then Lady Worthington-Brown. I was determined not to let my husband down so I went to a Charm School to learn how to be a lady. It was not easy for me as I was by then in my forties and all the other students had only just left school. But I stuck it out and ended up being a society hostess in London, entertaining the aristocracy and even royalty. Little did they know who I really was" she laughed "If they had only known! Henry and I enjoyed my secret and he said he was proud of me"

There was a long silence in the room when Her Ladyship had finished her story. As she sat there she pulled off her diamond earrings, unclasped her pearls, and pulled the rings from her fingers. She wrapped her jewels in her handkerchief and pushed them into the pocket of her cardigan.

"Now I am just an ordinary woman, no longer Her Ladyship. I want you to call me Maisie and to let me help in the housework. I am particularly fond of gardening and am more than willing to help grow vegetables for our table. I would be honoured if you would permit me to call you Bert and Dora. Will you let me do that?"

Dora put down her knitting and got up. She came and sat beside Her Ladyship on the settee. "Of course you can call me Dora" she said taking the other woman's hand "Thank you for telling us your story, it can't have been easy for you. I am so sorry for what has happened to you, losing your home like that to that horrible German brute. You are very welcome here and I am sure we are going to get along together really well"

"In that case" said Her Ladyship, now to be known as Maisie "I will begin as I mean to go on, and I am going to make us all a nice cup of tea"

With that she got up and disappeared into the kitchen. Higgs was still sitting upright on his chair. He seemed to be in a trance and it was Dora who pushed his pipe into his mouth and lit it for him.

An accident on the road to Newport

Issy and her brother Jack raced each other as they pedalled their bicycles along the deserted road from their farmhouse home to Newport. As they rounded a bend they saw another cyclist coming towards them on the other side of the road, it was a German soldier. To their horror his front wheel hit a stone in the road and he came off his bike. He flew over the handlebars and landed a few feet away from the siblings.

Issy leaped off her bike and ran to the man who was trying desperately to get up. He was lying on his side with one leg twisted awkwardly under him, and he had blood pouring from a gash on his forehead. Issy put a restraining hand on his shoulder "Don't try to get up" she told him, "I think you have broken your leg"

The young man peered up at her, clearly not understanding a word she had said.

She looked up at Jack who had come to stand beside her "Ride quickly to the big house down the road" she instructed, "there are soldiers billeted there. Go and get help"

While Jack rode off Issy pressed a handkerchief against the wound on the soldier's face and carefully tied a makeshift bandage round his head, using her scarf. The young man had quietened down and was no longer trying to get up. Issy cradled his head in her lap and spoke soothingly to him. If he did not understand her words he certainly understood the tone of her voice and he gradually relaxed and lay still.

Issy looked down at her patient. He was only a boy, probably not much older than herself, and she was just seventeen. Hard to believe that he was part of a hated occupying force. She felt very sorry for him. So far from home and lying hurt in the road. She could not think of him as the enemy, only as a fellow human being who needed help.

It was the autumn of 1941 and Germany had invaded the Isle of Wight just over a year after occupying the Channel Islands. Until then the war had seemed a long way off to the islanders, now they were in the thick of it. They looked across the Solent to the mainland which was so near but so far, and waited in vain for help.

After what seemed an age Issy heard a vehicle approaching, and then a military ambulance appeared round the bend, followed by a German staff car. An officer jumped out of the car and helped Issy up as the ambulance men came to the aid of the injured soldier. With quiet efficiency they tended their patient and gently placed him on a stretcher. They soon had him in the ambulance and were speeding off to their military hospital in Newport.

Issy and Jack watched all this going on, wondering what to do next. As soon as the ambulance had departed the officer spoke to the pair in perfect English.

"I want to thank you for your prompt action" he said "If you had not been there I cannot imagine how long that young man would have been lying in the road. You probably saved his life. You are Good Samaritans. Many people would have passed by and left a German soldier lying injured"

"We could not leave him" Issy replied, remembering how she had seen the soldier as a boy rather than a soldier " I am glad we could help. Now we must be going. My brother will be late for school and I am already late for work"

"May I give you a lift?" the German offered

"No" snapped Jack rather too emphatically, dreading to think what his friends would think if he turned up at school in a German staff car.

"It's all right" Issy added, trying to soften Jack's abrasive manner "It's very kind of you, but we have our bikes"

Jack climbed on to his bicycle and hurriedly pedalled off leaving Issy standing with the officer.

"Is there anything I can do to show my appreciation?" he asked. "Could I come to your home and bring you a gift? Perhaps you would like some tea or sugar, I know there is a shortage of these things"

"No, that would not be a good idea" Issy protested, "I don't mean to be rude or ungrateful, but I could be regarded as a collaborator if I accepted gifts from you"

"Ah yes! I understand" the officer replied ruefully. "I tend to forget these things. I lived in England as a boy and went to school in London. Before the war the English were my friends and I find it hard to accept that I am now their enemy"

"I am sorry" Issy said, and meant it. The officer was charming and very good looking. She would like to have got to know him better.

"I have an idea" he announced "I would like to take you for a picnic. When I am free at weekends I pack a basket and drive to Freshwater Bay, then I walk on Tennyson Down and eat my lunch looking out at the beautiful view from the top of the hill. Would you come with me? You could meet me here on the road, it's very quiet and you would not be seen and I would drive you back here afterwards"

Suddenly Issy found that she wanted to go on the picnic more than anything else. Against her better judgment she nodded "Yes, I would like that" she replied, and before she realised what was happening a time and date had been arranged.

The officer clicked his heels and saluted her. As he helped her to climb on her bicycle he said "My name is Franz"

"I am Isabel" she replied "but everyone calls me Issy"

Otto, the boy soldier

Maisie was busily clearing weeds in the garden one morning when she was suddenly aware that she was being watched. There was a boy standing by the gate. She straightened up and smiled at him "Hello" she said "Can I help you?"

The boy blushed and was about to turn away but seemed to change his mind "Otto" he said.

"Otto?" Maisie questioned, unsure of his meaning.

"Me Otto" he repeated, jabbing a finger at his chest.

"Oh I see" Maisie laughed "I am Maisie"

"You English" was the response

"Yes" Maisie agreed.

"Me German" Otto informed her

"I realised that" was Maisie's reply. The boy was dressed in khaki shirt and trousers, and seemed to be some sort of a soldier but was not in full uniform. He was tall and skinny and had very blonde hair that flopped on to his face causing him to push it out of his very blue eyes with a nervous gesture. Long hair for a German soldier, thought Maisie.

"You teach me English?" the boy suddenly demanded.

Maisie was taken aback "I am not a teacher" she told him but he obviously did not understand.

With that he turned away calling over his shoulder as he went "Me be back"

Maisie watched him walk away "What was that all about?" she wondered.

Later that evening Maisie and the Higgs had just finished supper, thick vegetable stew followed by apples from their orchard, when there was a knock at the door. They looked at each other in alarm, who could be calling so late in the evening?

Higgs went to the door and called out "Who's there?".

"Franz von Ginsberg" was the reply "May I come in for a moment, please"

Higgs opened the door, it would not be policy to turn a German away. The young officer stepped inside, clicked hi heels and bowed to the women.

"I am sorry to intrude" he said "but | have something to ask Your Ladyship, something by way of a favour actually. I know we met previously in rather unfortunate circumstances, but I hope you will not hold that against me. I was just obeying orders – rather reluctantly I have to admit". He gave her such a charming smile she was completely disarmed.

Maisie looked at him in amazement. "What can I do for you?" she asked.

Dora pulled a chair up to the fire "Won't you sit down" she invited.

The young man sat "You are very kind" he murmured in acknowledgement.

"I believe you met a young soldier by the name of Otto, My Lady" he said, addressing Maisie.

Maisie nodded.

"I would like to tell you his story" the officer continued. "He was a member of Hitler Youth and when the invasion of the Isle of Wight began he somehow got drafted into the army by mistake. He is a big boy and looked like a man, but he is only sixteen years old. He should never have come here, and when his age was discovered he should have been sent home. Instead of that he was seconded to Oberst Rauch's household and put to work in the stables tending the horses brought to the island by the officer. The Oberst is a very keen horseman and Otto is very good with horses"

There was a pause "Go on" urged Maisie.

"Otto is homesick and lonely, the other soldiers tease him. He saw you in your garden and you reminded him of his mother back home. She, too, likes to work in her garden. I believe he asked you to teach him English"

Maisie agreed. "But I am not a teacher" she protested "I would not know where to begin"

"In any case" Dora butted in "It would not be seemly for Her Ladyship to teach a German"

"Madam" Franz chided "If your son was in a foreign land would you not like him to receive some small kindness to make life more pleasant for him.   Otto may be a German but he is only a child, he is not here from choice and he should not be here anyway. Is it too much to ask for a little charity for him?"

Dora looked suitable chastened. "Would you like a cup of tea?" she asked to cover her embarrassment.

"That would be very kind" smiled Franz, immediately easing the situation.

Dora went to put the kettle on and Franz turned again to Maisie.

"I have some books that I used when I was at school. They are just basic vocabulary books but I brought them with me to help any of my comrades who needed to understand something of your language. I could let you have them. What do you say?"

Maisie thought for a bit. She remembered the appealing way Otto pushed his hair out of his eyes, and how he had looked so dejected as he turned to leave her..

"Very well" she agreed "I will give it a try, but if it does not work out after a week or so, I will not continue"

"Thank you so much" the young officer murmured "You are so kind"

Higgs, who had been listening to all this decided to join in.

"Why do you not teach the boy yourself?" he asked "Your English is very good, you would have no trouble teaching him"

"Alas" Franz regretted "That would not be considered appropriate. Army protocol is such that an officer would not be permitted to show favour to a mere stable boy. I know that sounds harsh, but it is the way things are. I have overstepped the mark by agreeing to be intermediary for him, but I felt sorry for the lad when he asked for my help, and am annoyed that he has been kept here when he should have been sent home."

"It's all right" Maisie intervened "I understand, and I will help him, but I would not like it to be generally known."

So it was agreed that Otto would come to the lodge each afternoon after lunch, when he could get away unnoticed. He would work with Maisie for about an hour and that the lessons would be for a trial period of one month.

"I will inform the boy" Franz told Maisie and with a click of his heels and a bow, he was gone

Escape from Parkhurst

The truck delivering provisions to Parkhurst rumbled into the prison yard. Fred and Bill were helping to unload when Jim arrived on the scene. When all the goods had been unloaded Bill asked Fred to keep the driver talking while he and Jim scrambled on to the back of the truck and hid among some old sacks and boxes. Reluctantly Fred did as requested and attempted to ask the driver, who did not speak much English, when he would be bringing more provisions.

When he saw that the two soldiers were safely aboard the truck he said goodbye to the driver and the truck pulled out of the yard.

Bill and Jim held their breath while the driver stopped at the gate and the guards chatted with him. After what seemed an age the truck pulled out of the gate and set off down the road, back to the depot in Cowes.

After jolting along for some time the truck pulled into the side of the road and the driver got out. Bill ventured a peep over the side of the truck and whistled quietly to himself. "Look at that" he whispered "The driver is springing a leak up against a tree. Now's our chance to disappear while he is busy"

Jim looked out over the side of the truck and chuckled "Come on" he said "Let's scarper"

The two men climbed out over the side of the truck on the opposite side to where the driver was urinating, and ran across the road to hide among some bushes.

They watched as the driver returned and the truck sped off down the road.

"Now what?" asked Bill.

"I reckon we are not far from Northwood where my old teacher lives. If we head off across those fields" he said, gesturing vaguely in the direction of where he though Northwood might be. "We should be able to get there without being seen.

"We won't be missed until roll call, so we are reasonably safe at the moment" Bill said "We should arrive at your friend's house before dark though We don't want to be caught out after curfew".

The two friends set off, keeping a wary eye out for anyone who might see them. Luckily they arrived at their destination without mishap.

Harold was working in his garden, planting vegetables, when he heard a soft voice calling his name "Pssst! Mr Johnson" it called. Harold looked round and saw a man's face peering over the hedge.

"Who's there" he called in reply, and the rest of the man emerged.

"It's Jim, isn't it?" Harold questioned' vaguely remembering the face. "You were my pupil a few years ago. Weren't you"

Jim came through the gate followed by another man. They were both in British army uniform. Alarm bells rang in Harold's head "What are you doing here?" he questioned.

Realising that all was not well, and fearing that the men might be seen, Harold bundled them both indoors. "Now" he said when the front door was securely shut "What is this all about?"

Jim explained that the pair had escaped from Parkhust in the back of a truck that had been delivering provisions to the prison. He told Harold how they planned to try and find a boat to take them to the mainland.

Harold shook his head in disbelief, "You have not thought this through" he declared "Boats are not just lying around waiting for people to escape. Did you know that anyone trying to escape would be shot?"

Jim looked crestfallen "Well" he said "we are out now. There's no going back. We could be shot for escaping from the prison so we might as well go on and be shot for rowing over to the mainland"

Bill joined in the conversation. "We know we can't row across the Solent but we could go in a motor boat, if we could get hold of one"

Harold was very unhappy about the situation and rather annoyed at having been involved. However, he realised that he was stuck with the two fugitives, and he began to formulate plans in his head.

"You had better hide in my loft until I can find a way to help you" he announced "My loft has a separate room behind the chimney breast. Downstairs access to it has long since been plastered over and the only way in is by crawling round the chimney stack just inside the roof. You would be safe there, but not particularly comfortable"

The two men expressed their gratitude and allowed themselves to be shepherded up into the secret room. Harold gave them some blankets and cushions and found them a loaf of bread and some cheese to take up with them. They scrambled up into the loft and left Harold to puzzle out what to do next.

Harold decided that this was a problem for the 'Group'. They all wanted to do something useful so this might solve their problem. He would report to them at the meeting that evening.

A Blossoming Romance

Issy looked in her mirror and liked what she saw. Her glossy hair, now no longer plaited, fell in soft curls about her shoulders, her skin was clear and her blue eyes sparkled. Her looks were improving, she decided, and it was all due to being in love. She put a finger on the dimple in her cheek and remembered how Franz thought it was so attractive. He had kissed it tenderly when last they met, and Issy shivered pleasurably at the memory.

She and Franz now met regularly, sometimes having a picnic on Tennyson Down and sometimes for a secret meeting in the old, derelict barn near her home. She longed for these meetings and wished they did not have to be in secret. She could not regard Franz as an enemy but she knew that if her parents found out they would be furious. Franz was German and to them that was the greatest condemnation. Issy understood that because she hated the fact that her beloved island was subject to enemy occupation. She hated the restrictions, the shortage of food and the hardship of occupation, but nevertheless, she relished the chance that had brought Franz to her.

Franz said he hated the occupation and that the only good thing about it was the fact it had brought Issy to him. He had told her often how much he loved her and he had asked her to marry him when the war ended. As Issy gazed in her mirror she sighed "When would this terrible war end? What would happen when it did? Would she ever be able to marry her beloved Franz?

Her reverie was rudely interrupted by the strident sound of her mother's voice calling up the stairs "Issy. What are you doing? Come down here at once. You will be late for work"

Issy sighed again and made her way down for breakfast.

Plans to help the fugitives

The 'Group' were delighted to have the opportunity to do something positive and did not seem to worry about being put in the dangerous position of sheltering escaped prisoners of war.

Albert told them that one of his brothers, who had joined the British Navy before the invasion, had a fishing boat moored off East Cowes. His brother's wife lived there with her children and she would know where the boat was. Albert volunteered to find out if it was serviceable and if the two escapees could use it.

Albert set off the next day in search of his sister-in-law, Gracie. He arrived at her house just as she was returning from taking the children to school.

"Come on in" she greeted Albert, holding the door open for him "It's lovely to see you"

Over a cup of tea Albert explained his mission, and the hope that Gracie knew the whereabouts of the fishing boat.

Gracie frowned "Oh dear" she lamented "I'm afraid the boat is at the bottom of the sea. The Germans punched holes in the bottom to prevent it being used, and it sank. But I do know that my father has a dinghy hidden away in his garden shed. Maybe that is still seaworthy. Why don't you go and see him. He lives in Gurnard"

After a chat about old times Albert bid Gracie farewell and set off for Gurnard. He found Gracie's father where she had described and knocked on his door. The old man opened the door cautiously and peered out through the crack "Who is it?" he asked nervously.

Albert introduced himself and explained that Gracie had suggested he visited the old man. He could not see more than the old man's face which looked lined and had a three day growth of bristle round a toothless mouth.

."You'd better come in then" the old man invited "my name's Bert, by the way"

"I know" Albert replied "we met at the wedding when Gracie married my brother"

Bert did remember and greeted Albert more warmly as he ushered him into a tiny, untidy parlour.

Albert explained his mission and Bert listened intently. "I do have an old dinghy" he agreed "but I don't know what condition it's in. I hid it in my shed under a pile of old sacks. Shall we go and take a look?"

The two men made their way down the overgrown garden to a dilapidated shed that looked as if it would fall down at any moment. Bert dragged open the door with some difficulty and Albert peered inside. There was no sign of a boat.

Bert squeezed in through the half open door and pulled some sacking away to reveal the end of a small dinghy. With Albert's help he cleared the rest of the sacking and the pair examined the boat. It looked in surprisingly good condition and a careful inspection revealed no sign of damage.

Bert covered the boat up again and he and Albert returned to the house. Bert agreed that the two fugitives could have the boat but he was very doubtful about it taking them all the way to the mainland. "It's too far for them to row" he said "and I don't have an outboard motor for it. You couldn't get petrol for it anyway"

Albert took his leave of Bert saying he would return when he had spoken to the two escapees. "I think they would be willing to take a chance" he called to Bert as he made his way back down the garden path.

Bill and Jim were delighted with the news when Albert told them about the dinghy. Even when it was explained to them that it might not be capable of carrying them to the mainland their enthusiasm was undiminished.

"I'm willing to take a risk" Bill stated, looking at Jm.

"Me too" replied his friend "I'm game for it. It's worth a try and we can't stay here. So let's go"

Harold was listening to this exchange and shook his head "It's very risky" he said "Are you sure you want to take the chance?"

The two escapees were adamant and so plans were laid. Two nights later, under cover of darkness, Harold and Albert took the two ex-prisoners across the fields to Gurnard. They were introduced to Bert who showed them his dinghy.

Again it was inspected for damage and all agreed that it was seaworthy. In the early hours of the morning Albert and Harold helped the two fugitives to drag the dinghy the short distance to the beach. They pushed it into the water and waited to see if it would float. When they were satisfied that it was not going to sink, Bill and Jim climbed aboard and Albert handed them the oars.

"Do you both know how to row a boat?" Albert asked and both men vowed that they were excellent oarsmen. Albert guessed quite rightly that this was a lie, but he said nothing.

Harold handed Bill a compass and suggested that they made for the coast west of Southampton. He explained that it was the nearest point on the mainland and would be less fortified than the city "You don't want to be shot by our own side, do you?" he commented "they may be suspicious of a lone boat arriving from an occupied island"

Quickly and quietly the two escapees pulled away from the shore and Albert and Harold watched until they were out of sight.

"I hope we are not sending them to a certain death" Harold remarked.

"It was their own choice" Albert reminded him.

"I wish we could know if they arrive safely" Harold said.

"I don't think we will ever be able to find that out" was the reply.

The two men made their way back to Bert's house where they would spend the rest of the night before returning home after the curfew ended in the morning.

Punishing a collaborator

Jack had an errand to run for the 'Group. He had to take a package containing instructions to one of the members who lived in Newport.

He rode his bicycle into town, relieved that he met no opposition. He parked the bike outside St Thomas's Church and made his way into the dark interior. When his eyes got accustomed to the gloom he saw that there was someone kneeling in prayer in a pew near the back. He slipped into the pew behind the man and whispered "Pass me a hymn book please"

The answer came "There are no hymn books here Laddy" . It was the right response and he slid the package on to the seat next to the stranger. It was immediately taken up and stored away into an unseen pocket. Jack knew his mission was complete and without a word he quietly made his way out into the sunshine.

Jack stopped in the doorway of the church, amazed to see that during the short time he was inside a crowd had been gathering outside. There were several men dragging a young girl into the square between them and they were followed by an angry, jeering mob of men and women. The girl was pushed up against the wall and her head was roughly shaved while two men held her down. Her screams were stifled by a dirty rag being pushed into her mouth. As the hair fell from her head blood began to pour down her face mingling with her tears.

Jack watched in horror. "What's going on?" he asked a woman who was standing nearby, shouting obscenities at the poor unfortunate girl.

"She is a slut who was seen kissing a German soldier in a dark alleyway." she told Jack before returning to her shouting "Collaborator" she yelled "Dirty collaborator"

Suddenly the square was full of German soldiers in the uniforms of military police. The crowd hastily dispersed as a few men on the fringes of the crowd were arrested. The soldiers took their prisoners away, they had not noticed Jack in the doorway. They left the victim of the mob's wrath cowering on the ground by the church wall. Slowly she pulled herself up and began hobbling away, wiping the blood from her face with the dirty rag she had spat out of her mouth. As she passed Jack he saw to his horror that he knew her. She was a girl who had been at school with Issy.

Jack was so shocked by what he saw that he remained rooted to the spot for some minutes. At last he pulled himself together and went to retrieve his bicycle. As he pedalled home he was filled with a sense of guilt because he had done nothing to help the girl. He could not have saved her from her humiliation but he could at least have comforted her afterwards. The memory of her staggering along the street, all alone with nobody to help her, remained with the boy for a long time afterwards.

When he got home Jack told no one what he had seen, but the event was to come back to haunt him a few months later.

Lost at Sea

Bill and Jim rowed away from the shore of the Isle of Wight feeling excited and elated. "We made it" Jim chuckled "we're on our way home"

Bill was a little more cautious "We're not there yet" he warned "There's a long way to go".

It was a very dark night and Bill was steering using the compass, but he was not at all sure they were going in the right direction. "We must get as near as possible to the mainland by dawn so we can see where we are"

"As long as we are a long way from the Isle of Wight, that's all I care" Jim chuckled.

The two men rowed strongly for about an hour then they began to flag. They were both undernourished and as they pulled out into the Solent the water began to get choppy. It was hard going and neither man was fit enough to cope.

"Let's rest for a while" Jim pleaded. His hands were sore and his muscles ached "I can't go on like this"

Bill agreed. He was exhausted and cold. "We'll let the boat drift for a while if you like"

The two men sat hunched up trying to regain their strength. There was no sign of the enemy so they felt relieved that they had got away unseen. But in the darkness there was no sign of the mainland either. They were both conscious that the Solent was heavily mined and they hoped that the dinghy would be too small to set any explosive device off.

Exhaustion got the better of them and they both dozed as they rested on their oars. Suddenly Bill woke up with a start, he realised that his feet were in water. "Wake up" he called to Jim, who did not react. "Wake up, Jim, we are taking in water"

In a panic Bill started looking around for something to bail out the water, but nothing came to hand. JIm had awoken by this and he, too, realised the peril they were in.

The two men desperately tried to bail out using their hands, but the boat was rapidly filling with water.

Suddenly a wave caught the boat and tipped it dangerously. Jim lost his hold on the oars and was thrown into the sea. In the darkness Bill desperately tried to locate his friend but it was useless. The water was now really rough and the little boat tossed about completely out of control. Bill clung on but he was too weak to hold on for long, and inevitably he, too was thrown into the sea.

The escape plan had failed and neither man managed to reach the mainland. Their friends on the island were left wondering what had happened to the two brave fugitives. There was no way they could ever find out.

London early 1943

Captain Meredith had just left the Prime Minister, Winston Churchill, in his Whitehall bunker. Churchill had sent for him because of his concern for the Isle of Wight. He did not like having the Germans literally on his doorstep. "It's too close for comfort" he complained to the young officer.

Captain Meredith, who worked for MI5, had been instructed to send an operative to the island to find out all he could about the occupying force. Churchill wanted to try re-capture the island but was uncertain how it could be achieved. There were no spare troops available to mount a rescue and, anyway, nothing was known about the strength of the occupying army.

The Captain walked back to his Head Quarters deep in thought. As he walked a plan was formulating in his mind. He knew just the man to send to the island, and on his return to his office he started to put his plan into operation.

A New Arrival on the Island

One dark night a submarine surfaced silently off the coast of the Isle of Wight near East Cowes. A rubber dinghy was lowered and two men climbed aboard. They rowed the dinghy to the shore and one man clambered on to the Esplanade, the other returned to the submarine. The man on shore watched as the dark shape submerged, and he was left alone on the island.

Dressed all in black he merged with his background. It was a risky operation but so far so good. There was nobody around as he made his way towards the road leading to Newport. Keeping to the shadows he walked towards his goal. He was surprised how quiet it was, he had expected to see military patrols, but none appeared. After some time he arrived at his destination, a small cottage set back from the road.

Harold was alarmed to be woken from a deep sleep by a persistent knocking at his front door. He climbed out of bed and opened the window, all was dark and he could see nothing. He cautiously made his way downstairs and, making sure the chain was in place, he opened the door a crack.

"Who's there?" he asked as he stood behind the door.

"It's Mike" came the whispered reply, "Your old pal Mike Hardcastle. Let me in, it's freezing out here"

"Mike Hardcastle!" exclaimed Harold "How did you get here?"

"Never mind how I got here" was the rather irritable reply "just let me in please"

Harold closed the door and released the chain then he opened it again and Mike slipped inside.

Mike and Harold had been friends for many years, ever since they served together in the army during WW1. Harold stared at his visitor in disbelief. He was thinking "Oh no! Not again" as he had only recently seen off his previous uninvited guests.

"It's good to see you, Mike" Harold greeted, trying to sound convincing " but very unexpected. Come in and tell me how you managed to get on to an occupied island in the middle of a war"

Harold lit the fire, poured his friend a stiff drink and waited for an explanation.

"I was brought to the island by submarine" Mike began "I am an agent with MI5 and I have been landed here to find out what is going on. I have radio equipment and I am to send messages back to HQ reporting on enemy activity."

He paused to sip his drink. Harold studied his friend as he waited for him to resume his story. He remembered Mike as a plump young man with dark hair a little to long for the fashion of the day. Now he saw a changed man. Mike had lost weight and was now lean and muscular. His hair was cut very short and his skin was well tanned. Harold wondered if he had been overseas in a warmer climate than the one he was suffering on the Isle of Wight.

"I need a place to hide for the next couple of weeks or so. I remembered that you live on the island and I know I can trust you. Would you be prepared to let me stay here with you? I know it's a lot to ask, but it is important to the war effort"

"Well – er!" was all Harold could say, he was speechless.

"I would never transmit from your cottage" Mike reassured his friend. It's just a case of somewhere to lie low"

"Of course you can stay here" Harold replied. He felt excited to be involved "What's more I may be able to help you" He told Mike of his involvement with the 'Group'

Harold knew he could trust Mike and he wanted to help. He remembered the good times he and Mike had enjoyed between the wars. During their holidays from the school where they taught they had travelled all over the world together. Sometimes they would take Harold's old car and tour Europe, and other times they were content to take the train up north and explore the delights of the Yorkshire moors or the beauty of the Lake District. They had not seen each other for several years so there was much catching up to do.

Eventually they came to the subject of the war and the efforts of the 'Group' to think of something to do to help the war effort. Mike was interested and wanted to know more. The two friends sat talking until it was nearly dawn. Harold decided that he could put a camp bed up in the secret loft where the two escaped prisoners of war had hidden, and make a reasonably comfortable and safe hideaway for his guest.

Where are our boys?

The Barry family were just finishing breakfast when Pa Barry came bursting into the kitchen, his face red with anger.

"That good for nothing boy, Albert" he stormed "Where is he?"

"What do you mean, Pa?" asked Ma, "Come and sit down and have a cup of tea. You look as if you are about to have a heart attack"

She pulled Pa over to the table and pushed him on to a chair. She poured him a strong cup of tea and waited while he sipped the boiling liquid.

"Albert" he said at last, "That useless piece of ……"

"Pa!" warned Ma "No swearing in front of the children"

"Albert has not turned up this morning" Pa told them, calming down at last. "I have had to do all the milking single handed. He has really let me down this time. I will sack him when he turns up again"

"Now don't be silly, Pa" Ma cautioned "There must be a good reason. He is usually so reliable. You can't sack him now. You wouldn't be able to find a replacement. If you sack him you would be cutting off your nose to spite your face. In any case if it had not been for the German invasion you would have lost him anyway, he would have been called up to join the army months ago. So at least give him a chance to explain himself."

Pa thought about it for a moment "You're right" he agreed at last "Jack run down to Albert's cottage and find out what has happened"

"Oh no!" Jack moaned "I'll be late for school"

"Not if you run both ways" Pa told him "Stop arguing and just go – now"

Reluctantly Jack got down from the table and made for the door. He ran as fast as he could across the fields and arrived, panting, at the cottage door. He knocked loudly "come on – come on" he said to himself as he waited for someone to answer the door..

After what seemed an age the door opened and Albert's mother stood there still in her long, flannelette nightdress, with a shawl pulled tightly round her shoulders to keep warm. Her eyes were red with weeping.

"Where's Albert?" Jack gasped, trying to get his breath back.

"Gone" wailed the mother, and she burst into tears.

"Gone" repeated Jack "Do you mean he's dead?"

"No" sobbed the distraught woman "Taken by the soldiers"

"What do you mean?" asked Jack.

"Soldiers came early this morning and arrested Albert" the old woman whispered "They had other men with them as well. They were all lined up by the gate, and when they took Albert they made him join the line then they marched them all off".

"Where have they gone?" Jack wanted to know. The woman did not answer, she turned away and went back in to the house.

"I'll get Ma to come and see you" Jack called through the letterbox. "She will look after you"

He turned and ran as fast as he could, back across the fields to his home. Pa was waiting for him by the farm gate.

"Well?" Pa called as Jack came near. "What excuse did Albert give?"

"Albert's not there" the boy told his father "He has been taken by the Germans"

He ran on to call his mother "Ma, Ma" he called as he came in to the kitchen "Albert has been taken away by the soldiers. The old lady is really scared. Will you go to her?"

"Of course" replied Ma, taking off her apron "I'll go at once. Where have they taken Albert?"

"Don't know" was the reply as Jack grabbed his school satchel and ran to get his bike. With any luck he would still be in time for school.

Ma pulled on her coat and hurried out to the road. As she walked along she met other women, all making their way towards the village. They had all had sons or husbands taken away that morning.

Ma called at the cottage and brought Albert's mother out to join the other women. They came up to the inn where the Publican was standing outside watching their arrival.

"They took my cellar man" he told them "I don't know where they have all gone"

AT that moment a German staff car pulled up and Franz climbed out

"What is going on?" he asked, but nobody answered. All the women were shouting and crying, and he could not make himself heard.

"Silence" he yelled, to no avail.. He pulled out his revolver and fired a shot into the air. The chattering stopped and there was a shocked silence. All eyes were on him. The sound of the shot brought soldiers running from the nearby barracks, all had their guns raised and pointing at the women, who looked as if they would panic at any minute.

Franz spoke to the soldiers in German and they lowered their guns but still stood confronting the terrified women.

Franz turned to the crowd "Now" he said "What is going on here?" It was Ma who explained about the arrest of the young men.

"I will not tell you where your young men are" he shouted "but I can assure you they will come to no harm. They will be helping the war effort, they will not be hurt."

"Helping the war effort" scoffed a voice from the back of the crowd "you mean helping the Germans. That's not helping, we want you out, we don't want to help you".

Franz ignored the comments. He sent the soldiers back to their barracks and ordered the women to disperse. Reluctantly they began to move away in ones and twos until they had all gone home. Franz got in his car and sat there for a while "What are we doing here?" he thought to himself "We should not be here on this island. We are here to satisfy the whim of the Fuhrer. We are not fighting a war, we are frightening old women and arresting boys to do our dirty work. When will it all end?" Sadly he turned on the engine and drove off down the road to Newport.

Later that evening the 'Group' met in the Barry's kitchen. Harold had news for them.

"Mike Hardcastle has found out what has happened to the young men taken away this morning" he announced, "Mike will not come here himself as he feels it best that none of you see him. He does not want to compromise you"

"Where are the lads?" Ma wanted to know. "Are they safe? I have heard of Germans arresting men and then shooting them"

"No, they are being set to work" Harold told them. "Mike came here because British spies had found out that Hitler has plans to make the Isle of Wight his

Head Quarters when he invades Britain. Mike was sent here to discover more. He has found out that Hitler plans to make Osborne House his base and that is where the lads have been taken"

"Why?" Pa wanted to know "What are they going to do there?"

"I am just coming to that" Harold continued "Apparently Hitler is coming to the island on a visit and the lads are going to make a runway in the grounds of Osborne House so he can land his plane there"

"I don't see why he would want to do that" said Ma "There are plenty of airfields on the island. Why would he want to build a special one?"

"He would want to land as near as possible to the house to avoid any sabotage. He is always in fear for his life"

"So he should be" Pa exploded "I'd kill him myself if I could get near enough".

"That's exactly why he would want to land in the grounds near the house" Harold pointed out. "Don't ask me how Mike found out, but he told me that the boys are to be kept prisoner in the grounds while they build the runway, and will not be let out until after Hitler has gone away again. So we will not see them for many months, but at least they are safe".

"And when is this dreadful monster coming here?" asked Ma "The cheek of it – we don't want him on our island"

"Probably in two or three month's time" Harold speculated "I don't really know, but I guess it will take that long to build the runway, and he won't come until it's ready"

There were all sorts of suggestions for sabotaging the runway but Harold held up his hand for silence "That is exactly how you can endanger the lives of our lads." He accused "Do you really want to do that?"

There were mumblings in the Group, "Think it through" Harold continued "Our hands are tied. We must not do anything to bring the wrath of the enemy down on our boys

Preparations for a very important visitor

Count Heinrich von Openheimer, a tall, blonde man with a military bearing and a haughty attitude enhanced by the monocle that he wore, giving his right eye a piercing stare that terrified his underlings, was second in command to Oberst Rauch. He really believed that he should have been the commander of the occupation forces, but Rauch was an old friend of the Furher, and so Heinrich had been bypassed. He was somewhat appeased when he was put in charge of preparing Osborne House to be Hitler's Headquarters when Britain had been conquered.

Heinrich loved Osborne House, he felt it was a fitting residence for a man of his importance and he began his task by commandeering the best rooms in the house for his own apartment. He had the rooms decorated and then he moved all the best pieces of furniture, from all over the building, into his own cosy little abode.

Only when he was comfortably settled did he begin the task of making preparations for Hitler. He did not actually believe that Operation Sealion would ever be successful, so he felt that there was no urgency to get the job done.

Heinrich's complacency was rudely shaken when there was a knock on his door one morning, and a young soldier came in bearing a message from Oberst Rauch. He took the paper from the young man and went pale when he read the contents.

The young soldier stood to attention watching the officer's face. Heinrich glared at him "Well. What are you waiting for?" he snapped.

"I am to take a reply to the Oberst" the young man stammered, being rather shaken by Heinrich's aggressive stare.

Heinrich snatched a piece of paper from a pad on his desk and hastily scribbled "*Message received and understood*". He pushed it into the soldier's hand ordering him to get out, which the young man hastily did with a click of his heels and a Nazi salute, which was not returned.

Heinrich read the message again and swore under his breath. It told him that the Oberst had received a notification that the Furher's planned visit to the Isle of Wight would take place as soon as the landing strip could be made ready in the grounds of Osborne House. Heinrich knew that a task force was already in the grounds, about to start the work. He had not considered that the visit would actually take place so soon

Heinrich sent for his secretary. "Call a meeting of all my officers" he ordered "We will meet later this morning to discuss plans for receiving a very important visitor". The meeting set everyone in a flurry. The officer in charge of making the runway reported that nothing had been started yet, but that the task force was ready to start work. The officer in charge of renovation of the house reported that, other than Heinrich's quarters, nothing had been set in motion, and the officer in charge of the kitchen had nothing to say at all.

Heinrich was aghast. He felt really wrong-footed. He began shouting at everyone in an effort to pass the blame on to others. But the others just regarded him with expressions of disdain. BY the end of the meeting plans had been made in abundance and the officers went off to put the work into operation.

Oberst Rauch further dismayed Heinrich by sending another message saying that the Furher had expressed a wish to sleep in Queen Victoria's bedroom.

Heinrich sent for his secretary again, "Which one of the many bedrooms in this house was Queen Victoria's" he asked.

The secretary looked perplexed, "I have no idea" he replied

"Then find out" Heinrich shouted "and be quick about it"

All the secretary's efforts were in vain. Nobody knew which room had been the Queen's. All the regular staff at Osborne House had been dismissed when the Germans took over and so it was impossible to find the answer.

"I have an idea" the secretary told his irate boss, "If we don't know which was Queen Victoria's bedroom, we can be reasonably certain that the Furher does not know either".

"Get to the point" Heinrich barked.

"We could put Herr Hitler in any bedroom and he would believe it was the one he wanted" was the reply.

Heinrich thought about this and then he smiled "You are absolutely right" he laughed "Well done you"

The secretary was so amazed by this unaccustomed praise that he was stunned into silence.

Heinrich selected a bedroom with a fine view of the garden but on the opposite side of the house to the view of the mainland. "Just to be on the safe side" he announced.

"Do you think a sniper with a long range lens might take a pot shot at the Furher?" somebody asked.

"Doubtful" was the reply "But it's better to be safe than sorry"

A selection of artefacts was then found from various locations in the house. Things like a photograph of Prince Albert, a silver dressing table set engraved with the royal coat of arms, and bed linen embroidered with 'V.R' . These were arranged round a great four-poster bed, and they made an impressive array. Heinrich was satisfied that the room was then suitable for a Queen, and therefore suitable for the Furher.

At last he felt ready to receive the very important visitor to the island.

Prisoners at Osborne House

There were twenty five young men rounded up and marched to Osborne House that morning. They were all nervous, wondering what was to become of them. They were given no explanation when they were arrested, and they had no idea where they were going on the long walk to Osborne House.

Eventually they turned into the gates of the estate and were waved through by the sentries standing guard. They were escorted to a patch of ground, some distance from the house and shown several large tents, lying on the ground. An English speaking officer joined the party and instructed the young prisoners to erect the tents. They looked at each other in amazement – how on earth would they do that?

Luckily one of the youths who had been a Boy Scout had some knowledge of tents and was able to help the others sort out the bits and pieces of tenting, pegs, poles and ropes. It took them all morning but, at last, they had the tents in place and they were then issued with bedding, pots and pans and other necessities. They still had no idea why they had been brought here.

At the end of the morning some German soldiers came and gave the youths bread and a bowl of soup each. They hungrily devoured their lunch and then lay on the grass relaxing until the English speaking officer returned.

The prisoners were lined up and told to stand to attention. None of them had any military training and were at a loss as to how they should stand. For the next hour they were drilled by a fierce German soldier who put them through their paces. By the end of the afternoon they all had a pretty good idea of how to behave on parade.

That evening they were given food for their supper consisting of a thin stew, which they ahd to cook for themselves, followed by bitter coffee which they hated. Then they were told to bed down for the night in the tents. They still had no idea why they were there.

They were woken early the following morning and drilled yet again before breakfast of bread and more of the disgusting coffee. Then they were lined up to wait for the officer to come and give them instructions. At last they discovered the reason for their arrest. They were there to make a runway suitable for a light aircraft to land in the grounds of Osborne House. They were not told why this was necessary.

They began by levelling out a strip of ground a little nearer the house than their makeshift camp. They were supervised by two German engineers who marched up and down and hit anyone slacking off.
They worked all that day and the next day too. In fact it took them nearly a week to get the ground flat enough to lay concrete on top.

Concrete mixers were then produced and the supervisors showed their prisoners how to mix concrete and spread it on the ground. Again it took them the best part of a week to complete the task.

They worked hard each day and slept well at night. They were treated reasonably well as long as they kept working, and they were fed regularly. The food was not to their liking, but they were so hungry they ate it anyway.

By the time the landing strip was ready the young prisoners had been held in the grounds of Osborne House for over two weeks, and there was no sign that they were going to be released. When their task was complete two very senior-looking officers came to inspect the landing strip and pronounced it satisfactory. The youths looked hopefully towards their guard, was he about to release them?

The answer was 'no'. Instead they were marched to the house, given mops and brooms, and told to clean the steps and the entrance hall. Then there were windows to clean and the gravel driveway to be raked. Several more days passed and still they were held prisoner and made to work.

Then, one morning, there was great excitement among the German soldiers. Something important was about to happen. The young prisoners were woken up and told to stay in their tents. Guards were posted outside to prevent anyone leaving. Albert, who had become something of a leader among his companions decided to try and find out what was going on.

Albert had found a piece of broken glass buried in the ground when he was helping to make the runway.

He had hidden it in his mattress, thinking that one day it would come in useful as a knife. That day had arrived. Albert carefully cut a small hole in the tent. It was facing the landing strip which he could see quite clearly through the trees. He lay on his bed peering through the hole and giving a running commentary to his friends.

Nothing happened for an hour, then he heard the sound of an aeroplane coming nearer. His patience was rewarded when he saw a small plane coming in to land on the newly made runway. The plane landed and taxied to the end nearest the house.

Albert watched as soldiers lined up making a guard of honour along the path from the runway to the house. The door of the aircraft was opened and steps were pushed up to it. The soldiers stood to attention. Then Albert saw a small figure come out on to the steps. He could see quite clearly as the figure gave the Nazi salute. The soldiers saluted back "Heil Hitler" they chorused. The man on the steps seemed to be making a speech, but Albert could not hear what was being said. It would have been in German anyway.

"Blimey"" he suddenly exclaimed.

"What is it? What is happening?" his companions were anxious to know.

"It's old Adolf" Albert whispered "Hitler is out there. I can see his black hair and his funny little moustache."

"So that's why we had to build that runway" somebody exclaimed "It was for him, the little swine."

"I wish I'd got a gun" somebody else said "It would be easy to take a pot shot from here"

Albert was watching, fascinated "He is so small" he told the others "I thought he would be big, but no, he's quite small. To think that such a little pipsqueak could cause so much trouble in the world." He shook his head in disbelief.

"Here, let me see" said one of the youths, trying to push Albert out of the way.

"Too late" Albert told him "Hitler has come down from the plane and they are taking him to the house"

The youths were silent, horrified to think that Hitler was here on the Isle of Wight, and they had helped to make it possible for him to come.

"It's hardly our fault" Albert consoled them "We didn't have much choice, did we?"

Hitler remained on the island for two days, staying mainly in the house. The prisoners were kept in their tents most of the time that the Fuhrer was at Osborne, inly being allowed out occasionally, but kept well away from the house by their guards.

On the third day they were kept in and heavily guarded. Realising that something was happening Albert took up his position by his spy hole. Late in the morning he saw a guard of honour lining up along the runway and, sure enough, Hitler was soon seen being escorted to the waiting plane.

Albert gave a running commentary to his friends, telling them that the Fuhrer was climbing the steps into the plane. Then he turned and gave the Nazi salute before stepping inside. Then there was a rousing cheer from the German guard, accompanied by raspberies blown by the British lads (luckily unheard outside) and the plane slowly began to move down the runway. The lads inside the tents heard it as it took off and climbed into the sky above the Solent.

"Where are our fighters when we need them?" Albert whispered "What a wonderful opportunity to knock old Adolf out of the skies" But all remained silent and the plane carrying Adolf Hitler made its was safely back to France.

Albert and his friends hoped that now the purpose of their capture was completed, they would be released. This did not happen. The lads were held at Osborne House indefinitely. They were set to work in the grounds and in the house and became sort of unpaid servants to the Germans residing there.

"I'm sure this is against the Geneva Convention" one of the lads complained. The others wanted to know what he meant and he explained the terms of the agreement.

"Well we ought to complain" somebody suggested.

"Who should we complain to?" another lad wanted to know.

"We could try complaining to Adolf" Albert joked "I am sure he would be very sympathetic. Shall I write to him?"

"Ha ha!" somebody exclaimed, pushing Albert off the end of his bed.

Albert climbed back on to his bed "No, seriously" he said "We will just have to grin and bear it. Nobody's going to listen to us. Anyway its not too bad here, so we will just have to wait and see what happens".

The young men remained in captivity in the grounds of Osborne House until the Germans pulled out two years later.

Hitler's visit

It seemed to the officers stationed at Osborne House that the Furher was slightly nervous. During his stay on the Isle of Wight he kept looking towards the mainland. Could it be that he could feel Churchill's eyes boring into him from across the Solent?

This was the Furher's first, and only time on British soil, and perhaps he could feel the hostility in the air. He knew he was on enemy territory, and that the enemy was far from beaten.

During his stay he remained in the grounds of Osborne House, refusing all offers to show him round the island. The only people he met were the soldiers detailed to form a guard of honour on his arrival. As he alighted from his plane he noticed the tents behind barbed wire by the side of the runway. He was told that they were the living quarters of the task force who had built the runway, but was not told that the men involved were islanders. None of the other members of the occupying force were invited to meet him. In fact none of them even knew he was on the island.

Oberst Rauch and his staff were invited to a banquet on the second evening of the Furher's visit and Franz was included in the invitation. He did not really want to go and he hated every minute of the evening.

Franz sat at the great table in the huge dining room of Osborne House, and watched Hitler with interest. He was firmly of the belief that the Furher was insane. "How could such a man rule a great nation like Germany?" he wondered "Why do we not pull him down and destroy him?" But he knew why – the powerful followers of Hitler kept him in position because he enabled them to accrue vast wealth. Their own power was dependant on his and they would allow nothing to spoil that. Anyone who attempted to oust the Furher was brutally done away with. The only people who could bring Hitler down were the allies, and they were having a difficult job doing so. Franz offered up a silent prayer that the allies would succeed in the end. He felt embarrassed by his own disloyalty, but he wondered how many others round that table had the same thoughts.

In actual fact most of the soldiers forming the occupation force were rather enjoying it. Like those occupying the Channel Islands they were safely away from the fighting, and although the islanders were passively hostile, they posed no threat to the Germans. To most of the troops the job of occupying the Isle of Wight was a bit like a working holiday.

Hardship for the Islanders

The occupation of the Isle of Wight was beginning to hit hard. The Germans had provisions delivered by ship, but they did not share them with the Islanders. Food was beginning to run short. Shops, unable to stock their shelves were beginning to close down. So it was that the 'Group', at last, came up with an idea for a useful activity, they would organise food distribution.

Pa Barry decided to use one of his barns as a distribution centre. He would collect vegetables, eggs and milk from local farmers and sell them to local families. He would also arrange for the slaughter of animals to provide meat. The idea was to form a sort of co-operative among the farmers, and the idea was a success. As long as supplies lasted all would be well, but there was a need to plan for the future when provisions once again became scarce.

Tea and sugar quickly ran out and resourceful Islanders found a way of using honey to sweeten their food, and instead of tea they drank coffee made from acorns. Bread, butter and cheese were unobtainable and the main diet consisted of potatoes and vegetables. Fruit was plentiful in season from the orchards and hedgerows on the island. The Islanders went hungry but they did not starve.

Harold came up with another idea for the 'Group', a very risky one, he suggested they plan a robbery. They would break into one of the German's warehouses by the harbour in Cowes and steal provisions that were stored there. Ma Barry looked shocked, fearing for the safety of her family., but the rest of the 'Group' were very interested.

Pete was particularly enthusiastic "It's about time we did something to hurt the Bosh" he said "They have plenty of food and they watch us struggling for survival. I vote we take some of their food from them and let them go hungry for a change"

"I agree" responded his son, "I am all for that"

The 'Group' now depleted by the absence of Albert, consisted of Pa Barry, Harold, Pete and his son, John, plus Ma Barry and Jack. Pa Barry looked at the men. Not an inspiring bunch, he thought. Would they be capable of mounting a raid on a German warehouse? He doubted it.

"Whatever we plan" he said, not wanting to dampen the enthusiasm, "Ma and Jack are not to be included. I am not having women and children put I danger"

Much to Ma's relief the men agreed. Jack would be disappointed when they told him he was to be left out, but he would have to put up with that. There was no way she would allow him to participate, and was glad to know that Pa was on her side.

The 'Group' broke up and Harold, Pete and John shuffled off to make their way home across the fields.

"Everyone think of some ideas to put to the rest of the group at our next meeting" Pa advised. "Between us we will come up with a plan".

A Shock for Jack

One afternoon when Jack came home from school he met his father at the gate.

"Come into the barn for a minute, Jack" Pa said, pulling the boy across the farmyard.

"What's the mystery?" Jack asked once they were inside the barn.

"A message from the 'Group" was the reply "We have a job for you"

Jack was excited, he had wanted to be used by the 'Group' more often but so far only a few missions had come his way.

"We have heard rumours that a local girl is meeting a German soldier in the old, derelict barn just along the road from here"

"I know where you mean" Jack replied "What do you want me to do about it?"

"Apparently they usually meet early in the evening, round about 6.00pm or thereabouts." His father informed him "we want you to get there a bit before that this evening and keep watch. We want to know who the girl is, so report back to me when you see her. You had better go in for your tea now and tell Mum you are going out again with your pals. Then make your way to the old barn and hide until the soldier and his girl arrive"

Jack did as his father told him and was soon out again making his way to the old barn. He arrived in good time and took a look round. There was nobody in sight so he slid inside and climbed up a rickety ladder on to a half floor where hay was stored. There was a little hay still there, smelling very musty. Jack hid behind a bale where he had a good view of the barn door, but was sure he could not be seen.

He waited patiently, feeling rather uncomfortable with the old hay pricking his legs. He kept a wary eye out for rats because he could hear a rustling sound that he guessed came from livestock living in the hay bales.

Just after six o'clock he heard a car coming along the road. It came close and the engine cut out. A car door slammed and Jack heard footsteps coming towards the barn. The door opened and a German officer slid inside. He stood just below where Jack was hiding, and lit a cigarette. As the match flared Jack saw his face clearly, it was the officer who had come to collect the soldier who had fallen off his bicycle, and had thanked Jack and Issy for their help.

The Officer walked across to the barn door and propped it open, allowing light to flood into the barn. After only a few minutes Jack heard footsteps coming towards the barn. The Officer went out and soon returned followed by a girl. Jack could not see her clearly as she was masked by the man in front of her. The officer took the girl in his arms and kissed her. As they embraced the girl's cardigan slipped from her shoulders and, as she turned to pick it up, Jack saw her face – it was Issy.

Jack was so shocked he almost cried out. The girl was his own sister, what should he do? He remembered the scene he had witnessed in Newport, when a girl had been assaulted by an angry crowd and a rough man had shaved her head. He could not submit his sister to that.

Jack lay still behind his hay bale until the Officer and Issy left. He hid face to avoid seeing the passionate embraces between the pair and he covered his ears because he could not bear to hear the loving words they exchanged.

Jack waited for some minutes after he heard the car pull away and then he made his way home. Pa was waiting for him.

"Did you see them?" he asked as soon as they were alone. "Who was the girl?"

"I hid in the hay loft and I did see them" Jack agreed "but it was too dark for me to see their faces. Sorry, I don't know who she was."

Jack felt uncomfortable lying to his father, but he could not betray Issy.

"Well you will have to go back again and hide outside the barn so you can see them in the daylight" said Pa, sounding rather annoyed.

"Yes,'spose so" Jack reluctantly agreed. Whatever could he do? Somehow he must warn Issy without disclosing the existence of the 'Group'. How could he explain that he had been spying on her? He made his way home across the farmyard feeling as if his world was collapsing around him.

A Plan is Hatched

Each member of the 'Group' came up with a plan to rob the German warehouse. Each plan seemed to be more bizarre than the last but it was Pete who came up with an idea that seemed to be workable.

"I have a cousin who is a greengrocer in Cowes" he informed the others "His shop is just round the corner from one of the German warehouses. If we could break in and get some of the stored provisions we could take them to Sam's shop and hide them in his store room until it was safe to collect them and bring them home. "

"Why not bring them straight home?" asked Pa Barry.

"We could not carry heavy packages through the streets, we would need transport" Pete explained

"Point taken" agreed Pa nodding his head "and, of course, the Bosh would be looking out for the thieves. We would have to wait until the fuss died down."

"Ay, that we would" commented John. "We would need to bring a cart to transport the stuff from Sam's shop, and that would arouse suspicion"

"We are rather jumping the gun" laughed Pa "We are discussing how to move the goods but we have not yet come up with a plan for getting into the warehouse in the first place. We need to plan that before we go any further"

"I have thought of that" said Pete "we need to have a look at the set up round the warehouse. We must find out what guards are on duty and what sort of locks there are on the doors"

Harold had been silent up till then. "I can do that" he chipped in "I can speak to any guards in German and find out a bit about how well the warehouse is protected"

"Thanks, Harold" said Pa "we will wait until you report back and then we will formulate a plan"

The next day Harold made his way to Cowes and walked slowly past the warehouse. He noticed that there was a high wire fence all round it and that there was one German soldier standing by the gate. Just inside the gate he could see two German Shepherd dogs chained up outside a kennel.

He stopped beside the soldier and said 'Good morning' to him in German. The man looked startled, it was the first time an islander had spoken to him in his own language.

He looked at Harold suspiciously but did, at last, respond to the greeting.

Harold asked the soldier about the dogs. He wanted to know why they were chained up. He was informed that they were guard dogs and that they were released at night when they would run free in the yard, guarding the premises.

Harold then asked if there was no human guard at night, and was told that it was not necessary as the dogs were capable of frightening any intruder off. The soldier laughed and slapped Harold on the back. Harold laughed too and bade the soldier farewell. He walked off smiling to himself.

While he had been talking to the soldier Harold had got a good look at the gate behind him. He saw that there was a padlock attached to it. Easy to force, he thought. He also noticed that there was a broken window near the door to the warehouse. It should be easy to break in. Obviously the Germans did not expect anyone to make the attempt as they seemed to have made very little by way of security.

Harold reported back to the 'Group' telling them all that he had discovered.

Pa Barry looked thoughtful "I have some rat poison" he said "suppose we poison the dogs, that would enable us to get in safely"

John was horrified, "You can't kill dogs" he exploded "that's inhumane"

"Oh! Come on, John" Pa protested "the dogs would be casualties of war, killed in order to provide food for the island's children. Which would you prefer? Vicious dogs or starving children?"

John ws a well known animal lover. In fact it was his love of animals that had saved him being taken with the other young men when Albert was arrested. John had spent the night sitting with a pregnant sheep that was about to give birth and was in difficulties, so he had not been at home when the soldiers came to call.

"Put like that I suppose we have no alternative" John reluctantly agreed "but I don't want the dogs to suffer"

John gave in because he had a secret passion for Issy and he did not want to antagonise Pa Barry. His only hope of getting nearer to Issy, who persistently ignored him, was through her father, so he had to keep on his right side.

The others ignored John's canine sentiments and went on with their plans, which, by the end of the meeting, had been well formulated.

Mr Rosenberg Disappears

Maisie was making one of her rare visits to Newport. Like most of the islanders she had lost weight during the occupation and she wanted to take a skirt to the tailor to be altered and made smaller. New clothes were practically impossible to obtain so she was keen to preserve this old favourite.

She walked down Pyle Street where Mr Rosenberg's tailor's shop was situated, looking forward to seeing him again, he was such an amusing man and she always enjoyed a chat with him

When she reached his shop she had a terrible shock, the window was smashed and there was a sign chalked roughly on the door. It said 'JUDE'.

The shop was closed and there was no sign of life. She was just about to knock on the door when a voice called to her from across the street.

"It's no good knocking on that door" an old man called from a window opposite.

Maisie crossed the road and looked up at the man "Why?" she asked "Where is Mr Rosenberg?"

"They took him away" was the reply

"Who did" Maisie wanted to know "Who took him away and where has he been taken?"

"The soldiers came and took him" the old man told her "They came in the night and took the whole family"

"Not the children too?" Maisie was shocked

"The whole family" the old man said "They took all the Jews in Newport. I heard that they are to be taken to work camps in Germany. A terrible business and a bad day for the island. That man, Hitler, is evil, he causes great suffering. How can such a man wield such power, what is the world coming to?"

He coughed loudly and Maisie thought she saw a tear in his eye. Suddenly he closed his window and disappeared from view. Maisie looked round to see what had frightened him and saw two German soldiers coming towards her down the street. Luckily they were too far away to hear what the old man had said.

Maisie thought of the Rosenberg children. Mr Rosenberg was always talking about them, he was so proud of his teenage son who was top of his class at school, and his little daughter, Rachel, who was the apple of his eye. He worshipped his children. What was to become of them?

Maisie would like to have thanked the old man for telling her what had happened and she wished she could have bid him good morning. Sadly, she made her way home. What a terrible world we live in, she thought, echoing the old man's words, when is this awful war going to end?

The Raid on the Warehouse – Cowes, Christmas 1943

The raid took place on Christmas Eve because that is when the Germans celebrated Christmas. It was a very quiet night as all the islanders were staying indoors trying to keep warm, and the Germans were enjoying their Christmas feasts. Just before curfew Pete and John cycled down to Cowes and disappeared into Sam's shop. They were joined shortly afterwards by Harold.

The three men waited until just before midnight and then they made their move. First of all Harold made his way to the gates of the warehouse and whistled to the dogs who came running over to him, snarling and baring their teeth. Harold pushed two pieces of meat through the bars of the gate and watched while the dogs, who had been deliberately kept without food to make them more aggressive, hungrily devoured the morsels. They had ben liberally laced with rat poison.

After a few minutes one of the dogs went back to its kennel and disappeared inside. The second dog collapsed on the ground by the gate. Harold waited for a short while and then broke the padlock holding the gate shut, he pushed the gate open and slid inside.

Harold made sure the dog was dead and then he dragged it across to the kennel and eased it inside to join its companion. Satisfied that the dogs were not going to recover Harold then went back to the gate and whistled three times as a signal to Pete and John, who were watching from the door of the greengrocer's shop.

John came over to join Harold. He was pushing a wheelbarrow with its wheels covered in cloth so as not to make a noise. Pete joined them pushing a trolley, also with suitable muffled wheels.

Harold had no trouble breaking into the warehouse which seemed very inadequately secured. Once inside he lit his torch and examined the labels on the many boxes and crates stored there. "Lucky I speak German" he whispered to the other two who did not have a clue what the labels meant.

The three men decided they would take sugar, flour, coffee and salt because these were products in short supply to the islanders, and they would be easy to transport. Harold found what they needed and they loaded their haul on to the wheelbarrow and the trolley.

When they had all they could carry Harold went outside to make sure all was clear, then he beckoned first to John to come to the gate. Harold let him out and watched him reach the greengrocer's shop safely. Then he beckoned Pete who also reached the shop safely. Harold then returned to the warehouse and nipped inside to collect one more item that he had his eye on. He took a box of soap and carried it out before pulling the heavy door closed again. He made his way to the gate and was just going to go through when he heard the sound of raucous singing. He stepped back into the shadows and watched as two very drunk soldiers staggered past, holding each other up as they reeled along the road.

Harold sighed with relief when they passed by without noticing him, and he was able to join the others in Sam's shop. When they were all gathered inside Sam helped them hide the stolen goods, some among his vegetable and others down in his cellar. Then they all settled down for a very restless sleep on the floor of Sam's flat above the shop.

Early the following morning, as soon as curfew ended, Pa Barry harnessed his pony to the cart and drove along the road to Cowes. He arrived without incident and pulled into the yard behind Sam's shop. He had already prepared the cart by making a false bottom under which the stolen goods could be concealed.

All the goods were stowed away and then straw was strewn over the false bottom of the cart. Sam loaded several bags of potatoes on top of the straw and Harold climbed up beside Pa Barry ready for the journey home. Pete and John would cycle home later in the day.

It was a fine, crisp winter morning and the two men were enjoying the ride when, suddenly, a German staff car appeared round the bend coming towards them. The driver slowed down and waved Pa Barry to pull into the side of the road. Two German officers got out of the car and came towards the cart.

"Papers" one of the officers demanded. Pa and Harold produced their identity cards and waited while the man carefully examined them.

"Where are you going?" the soldier wanted to know.

"We are going home" was the reply.

"Where have you been so early in the morning?" the second officer questioned.

"We have been to Cowes to collect potatoes for our Christmas dinner" Pa told him.

The two soldiers walked round to the back of the cart and looked at the sacks stacked up there. One officer took out a penknife and slashed one of the sacks open. Potatoes rolled out on to the floor of the cart. Pa and Harold sat patiently waiting and holding their breath.

One of the officers said something in German to his companion. They both looked at their watches and turned to get back in their car. Harold and Pa watched as they drove off .

"Happy Christmas" Harold called after them but they were too far away to hear.

"Why did they hurry off like that?" Pa asked "I thought they would have wanted to ask a lot more questions"

"They were in a hurry" Harold told him "They are flying home and they needed to get to Bembridge airfield to meet their plane. It's lucky that they are leaving the island because when our robbery is discovered they might have remembered us and reported us to the authorities. We could have been suspects"

Pa agreed and suggested that they got home quickly. "We need to get the stuff unloaded and hidden away as soon as we can"

They set off again and the poor old pony had to run faster than he had ever done in his life. When they were safely home the pony got a carrot as a 'thank you'.

Within a few days all the local families had been provided with flour to make bread and cakes, and sugar to sweeten the cakes. Much needed salt was also a blessing and coffee was becoming a popular drink among a nation of tea drinkers.

Of course it was not long before the robbery was discovered and a search was made for the thieves and their stolen goods. Houses and shops were searched around the area of the warehouse. Sam's shop was practically taken apart but nothing was found. The same happened in other local shops, but likewise there was nothing discovered. The goods were far away and long since distributed, and the Germans, despite their suspicions, had to accept defeat.

Local residents feared reprisals, but were relieved when the whole affair blew over and was soon forgotten. They noticed that stronger locks appeared on the gates of German warehouses.

A Spy is Discovered

Jack had been wondering what to do about Issy and her German officer. His father was still pressing him to find out who the mysterious girl was and he was determined not to give his sister away.

His problem was just about to be solved in a very dramatic way.

Pa had sent him to spy on the old barn one evening and he was hiding outside among some bushes. He thought he heard sounds coming from inside the barn, but having listened very carefully , he decided it was either his imagination of perhaps some of those rats living in the hay.

After he had been waiting a short time he heard the sound of an approaching car, and then a German staff car pulled up and an officer got out. Jack watched him walk up to the barn and go inside. It was the man he had been expecting.

Jack came out of hiding and crept up to the door. He saw the officer standing by a ladder that lead up to the hayloft, he was lighting a cigarette.

Then a strange thing happened. The officer paused and looked up at the loft. "Who is there?" he shouted, but there was no reply. The officer began to climb the ladder to have a look up there. As he was about half way up a figure suddenly launched itself off the hayloft and landed on the officer knocking him to the ground.

The figure, which was a man that Jack thought he had seen before, was carrying a suitcase which he dropped as he fell to the ground on to the officer. The German grabbed at the bag and it came open spilling the contents on the floor. The man pulled it away from the German and ran out of the barn carrying the bag with what remained of its contents.

The German tried to get up but called out in pain. His leg was twisted under him and Jack guessed he had broken it. He was just wondering what to do when he heard footsteps coming towards the barn. Quickly he stepped inside and crouched in the shadows just in time as Issy came into view.

He watched as Issy came in. She saw her officer lying on the ground and rushed to help him.

"Oh Franz!" she cried "Whatever has happened. Are you badly hurt?"

She crouched down beside the German and they spoke in low voices. Jack could not hear all that they said but he did hear Issy say "I will go and get help".

She ran out of the barn and the officer lay back against the ladder and closed his eyes. Jack wondered if he had passed out.

The boy took the opportunity to slide out of the barn and take up his former position in the bushes. He looked around but there was no sign of the man who had knocked the German over.

Jack wondered what he should do. If he stayed hidden in the bushes whoever came to rescue the officer might find him and think he was involved in the attack. So he decided to come out of hiding and stand in the road, looking as if he had just happened to be walking along at that moment.

It was a wise move because a car came racing down the road and four German soldiers jumped out, their guns at the ready. They rushed into the barn, taking no notice of a boy walking down the road.

Of Issy there was no sign.

Jack made his way home and reported the events to Pa. He made no mention of Issy. Pa looked horrified and Jack guessed he knew more than he was telling. The boy suspected that Pa knew who the mysterious man was.

Issy was in the kitchen with Ma, helping to prepare the supper. Jack thought she looked very pale and she seemed to be rather agitated. He was not surprised.
Later as they were just finishing their meal there was an impatient hammering at their door. Pa went to inspect and came back into the kitchen followed by two German soldiers. "You will all stay in here" one of them commanded as he pushed Pa on to his seat by the table. "Guard them Heinz" he told his colleague while we search the house".

Heinz remained in the kitchen with his gun trained on the family, while the other soldier brought in reinforcements to search the house.

"What are you looking for?" Ma asked nervously as she heard trampling feet overhead. Heinz remained impassive, giving no indication that he had heard her. Probably he did not speak English.

After what seemed an interminable time the first soldier came back.

"Have you seen a stranger around here?" he asked.

They all denied having seen any such person.

"Anyone harbouring a spy will be shot" the German informed them "If you see anyone suspicious you must report them to the authorities immediately. Do you understand?"

Nobody spoke.

"Well do you? Answer me" the man demanded.

"We understand" Pa eventually agreed and the soldiers left.

"What was all that about?" Ma asked, she was shaking.

"It's alright, Ma" her husband reassured her "I think there has been some sort of an incident and the Germans are looking for a spy. I guess they are searching all the homes in the area. They found nothing here so we should be safe now"

They were safe but there was bad news for other families the following day. Notices were pinned up on trees and lampposts all around the area.

A German officer has been attacked and injured by a suspected spy. A search of the area has not revealed his whereabouts. It is believed that some local person is hiding this man. If he is not found by the end of this week one of the Englishmen working for us on the Osborne Estate will be shot. One of these men will be shot each day until spy is found. By order of the Commandant.

That night Pa crossed the fields to Harold's cottage.

"They are looking for Mike Hardcastle, aren't they?" Pa asked his friend.

"I know" Harold replied "What a dreadful situation. Mike came home yesterday evening in a dreadful state. He packed up all his belongings and left in a hurry. He only just got away in time and, luckily, when the Germans came searching there was no trace of him here"

"What had happened?" Pa wanted to know.

"Mike was hiding in a barn transmitting a message back to the mainland, when a German officer came in. He heard Mike up in the hayloft and went to investigate. Mike jumped on him and ran off, but he dropped his case with the transmitter in it. The officer managed to get hold of the Morse Code pad and Mike had to leave it behind. That is how they know he is a spy"

"You know that they are going to start shooting our boys one at a time each day until Mike is found"

Harold nodded.

"Well, what are we going to do about it? Do you know where Mike is?"

Harold shook his head "He could be anywhere" he replied.

"We can't let them kill our boys" Pa whispered, he was almost in tears.

"I know" Harold replied "But I can't think of what we can do to stop them"

"We have just five days to come up with something" Pa announced "Just five days before the killing commences"

As the days passed by the mood in the village became very sombre. The Germans had not found the spy and nobody had come forward to denounce him. People were looking at each other with suspicion and wondering who, among them. was harbouring a fugitive. Which of their boys would be the first to die if the spy was not found? By the fourth day anxiety had become terror.

Then an amazing thing happened. On the evening of the fourth day Mike Hardcastle presented himself at the German Head Quarters in Newport. He looked dirty and dishevelled and claimed he had been hiding in woods near East Cowes. He produced the suitcase with the remains of his radio in it, to prove who he was.

News quickly spread, the spy had given himself up. He knew that island boys were to be shot and he had surrendered to save them. It was a very heroic act.

Rumours were rife. People said that the spy had been taken to Parkhurst Prison and was to be tried by court martial there. They were correct, that is exactly what happened. "What about the Geneva Convention"? people asked. Would there not be strict rules about how the spy should be treated? Nobody knew the answer to that, but in the end they suspected that the outcome was not entirely legal, because two days later islanders were shocked when a notice went up outside Parkhurst Prison where Mike was being held. It simply said:

**A captured English spy has been tried and found guilty. He was sentenced to death.
This sentence was carried out by firing squad early this morning.**

No-one knew what had happened to the body and everyone was too frightened to ask, but a funeral service was carried out secretly in the village church the following Sunday.

Nobody noticed a German officer standing in the shadows at the back of the church. He was on crutches and his leg was in plaster.

A Note from Issy

Issy had started working late – or so she said. Instead of arriving home from the bank at five thirty in the afternoon it was now nearer seven o'clock in the evening. Ma Barry trusted her daughter and did not question the late hour.

Issy felt bad about lying to her mother but her circumstances had changed. Franz's broken leg was not healing well and he had been kept in hospital for many weeks. Issy had been visiting him there after work. She could not tell her family that, so she was forced to lie, and it went against the grain.

One evening there was a shock for her, Franz told her he was being sent home to Germany. He was to fly home the following week. She cried out in horror when he told her.

Franz took hold of Issiy's hands and held them tight. "Listen to me" he urged "I have a plan"

Issy gulped and looked into the young officer's eyes.

"I want you to come with me" he urged "I want you to come back to Germany and marry me"

He waited while she took this in.

"But that would mean leaving my family" she protested "They would never allow it"

"It would have to be a secret" Franz warned "Nobody must know what we plan"

Issy thought about what he had suggested "I need time to think" she whispered "Can I think about it and let you know?"

"You will have to let me know by tomorrow so I can make arrangements. Please, Issy" he begged "Please come with me. The war must end soon and we can make a wonderful life together in Germany"

Issy nodded "I will tell you tomorrow" she promised.

Issy agonised over the decision she had to make. She lay awake all night thinking about it. One moment she was determined to say no, but the next she changed her mind, she could not lose Franz. All night long she changed her mind over and over again. But in the morning she knew what she wanted to do.

That evening she went to Franz "I will come with you she said" and he heaved a great sigh of relief.

The flight was planned for the following Wednesday. Issy could only take a few things with her. She could not pack a bag so had to be content with what would fit in her handbag.

On Wednesday morning she went to work as usual. At 11.30 she complained of feeling unwell and asked to go home. The Bank Manager, Mr Wainright, looked at her pale face and agreed that she could go. "Will you be alright getting home" he asked "Shall I send for your mother to come and get you?"

"No thank you" Issy protested "I will be fine"

She put on her coat and picked up her handbag. "Goodbye, Mr Wainright and thank you" she said as she went out of the door.

As Issy left the bank a car pulled up outside and Mr Wainright thought he saw her getting in, but he could not be sure. Maybe she just walked round behind the car.

The plane took off at noon and Issy looked down at the Isle of Wight as they flew over her homeland. A tear came into her eye as she looked down "Dear island" she said to herself, I wonder if I will ever see you again"

That evening Ma looked anxiously at the clock "Issy is very late tonight" she said "Whatever can be keeping her?"

As it began to get dark, Ma became more and more worried. "I will just go up and close the curtains in Issy's bedroom" she announced.

A few minutes later Pa and Jack heard Ma scream. She came rushing down the stairs waving a piece of paper. "She's gone" Ma cried "Look at this"

She handed Pa the piece of paper. He read what was written on it and went and put his arm round Ma who was weeping uncontrollably.

Jack looked at the piece of paper, now lying on the kitchen table. He pulled it towards him and read:

Dear Ma & Pa
I have gone away with Franz.
We are flying to Germany and
we will be married there.
I am so sorry. I know how upset
you will be.
I love Franz and he is being sent home
because of his broken leg. I can't
bear to be left behind without him.
Please forgive me. I love you and
I love Jack. I am so sorry
Your loving daughter Issy

Jack pushed the paper back across the table. Oh! Issy" he thought "I will never see you again"

When Ma and Pa Barry had got over the shock of Issy's departure they began to think of more pracitical matters. What were they going to tell people? How would they explain Issy's departure?

In the end they decided to go and see Mr Wainright. When they arrived at the bank he ushered them into his private office.

"I know why you are here" he told them. "When Issy did not turn up for work this morning I looked in her desk and I found this note" He handed them a piece of paper. They read what was written on it.

"This is very similar to what she said in her note to us" Pa told the Bank Manager, "I don't know what to say. It is a terrible disgrace for our family"

"Those two young people love each other" Mr Wainright said "They are victims of this awful war. He is a nice young man, I have met him a few times and I liked him. In normal circumstances he would make an admirable husband for Issy. We must find a way to protect Issy's good name and, of course, to take any suspicion away from you"

Ma and Pa were very touched by the man's concern. The three of them talked the matter over for a long while and in the end they decided that Pa should simply go to the police and claim that Issy had disappeared.

None of them liked this solution, but agreed that it was for the best. Over the next few weeks the police searched for Issy and Ma and Pa felt embarrassed by the unnecessary effort they were putting into finding her. "What a waste of police time" Pa complained.

Ma was embarrassed by all the kind offers of help and the words of condolence received from friends and neighbours. "It's all a lie" she whispered to Pa "everyone is so kind and it's all for nothing"

"No it is not for nothing" Jack announced, much to their surprise "as far as we're concerned Issy is dead. We are never going to see her again, are we?" and he rushed up to his room where he sobbed silently into his pillow, mourning the loss of his sister.

Of course Issy was never found and after a while the whole matter was put on hold. As it happened events unfolded that put the whole matter of Issy's disappearance out of everybody's mind.

The Departure of the Germans

Franz was sent home to Germany in May, 1944. There was already concern among the occupying forces because of mysterious activity going on along the coast of the mainland. The German forces were aware that something was happening but they did not know what, and this made them nervous. The occupying force was a comparatively small army and they felt vulnerable, being so far away from the main German army.

On June 6th it became obvious what was going on. A large British force was seen crossing to France, and the D-Day landings had begun. German troops on the Isle of Wight saw, through their powerful telescopes, that a mighty army was descending on their colleagues in France, and they could do nothing about it. They also wondered how it would affect their position on the island.

A few days later a directive came through from Hitler, himself. The German troops were to evacuate the Isle of Wight and go to the assistance of the occupying forces in France. They were to depart immediately with the utmost urgency.

Troop ships were sent to various points around the island, and a fleet of planes landed on airstrips, to take the men and machines across to France. The Germans packed up hastily and were quickly on the move. The astonished islanders watched in alarm. Would the Germans do malicious damage to their property as they left? Would the islanders themselves be harmed? But all was well. The Germans were in such a hurry that they had no time to plan to harm the islanders or their property.

German fighter planes circled the Isle of Wight to keep off any attack from the British as the occupying army moved to board the ships and planes. There was a deep sense of fear in both Germans and islanders alike. It was a moment to great peril. The islanders instinctively kept indoors hoping for safety, as they watched the convoys of troops that seemed endlessly to pass their homes.

In Hill House Oberst Rauch realised that he could not take his beloved horses with him. Reluctantly he ordered one of his soldiers to go to the stables and shoot the animals. As it happened Otto overheard the order being given. There was no way he would allow the horses in his care to be slaughtered. He rushed to the stables, quickly saddled one of the horses and rode out of the stable leading the other horse by its reins. When the soldier arrived at the stables with his loaded rifle he found it empty.

Otto rode like the wind, urging the two horses on at a gallop. He rode into the woods and found a clearing where he could tether the horses. He kept watch throughout the day and well into the night, before falling into an exhausted sleep. When he woke in the morning he took the horses further into the wood, and there he remained until he was sure that all the Germans had left. Only then did he make his way back to Hill House, cold, hungry and worn out, he began to think of the position in which he found himself. He was a deserter from the German army and he was an enemy alien. He was terrified, but at least he had saved the lives of his beloved horses.

Hill House is restored to Maisie

Maisie and the Higgs watched as the Germans filed past the lodge. Cars and trucks full of soldiers and laden with their belongings drove past in what seemed an endless convoy. Maisie was keeping an eye out for Otto.

"What will happen to that boy?" she moaned

"Have you seen him go by?" asked Dora.

"Not a sign of him" Maisie replied "I don't suppose he had a chance to come and say goodbye. It all happened so quickly. I wonder what it was that made the Germans move out so rapidly".

"Something is happening on the mainland. I think there is a big offensive being launched against the German forces in France" Higgs informed the two women.

"Well it will be wonderful if they are really going" Dora commented "Freedom at last"

"Maybe" her husband grunted "but the war is not over yet. Perhaps the end is in sight. I sincerely hope so"

Maisie and Dora agreed, but Maisie was still anxious. She had grown very fond of Otto and regarded him almost as a son. She dreaded the thought that she may never see him again.

As the day wore on and the convoy of troops came to an end the watcher in the lodge drew the curtains and sat down to supper. Maisie was not hungry and sat toying with her food.

"Cheer up" Higgs encouraged "tomorrow we will go up to the house and see what damage the Germans have done. Don't worry, we will soon get it back to normal again"

"I'm not worried about the house" Maisie protested "It's the fate Otto that worries me. That poor boy. What will become of him?"

After a sleepless night Maisie came down to breakfast to see Higgs sorting through a bunch of keys.

"What have you got there? She asked

"Well" He replied "When the Germans took over Hill House I didn't give them all the keys. I kept a spare set hidden away so that one day you could get back in. That day has come, and after breakfast we can go up to the house and we will be able to get inside"

Later in the morning the trio walked up the drive and approached Hill House. It looked wonderful standing there in the morning sunlight. Maisie stood and looked at it. She was overcome with emotion. Here was her old home, its pale brickwork glowing in the bright sunlight and the wisteria making a vivid splash of colour as it shimmered in the light breeze.

"Oh my God! I think I am going to cry" Maisie stuttered "I never thought this day would ever come"

Dora put an arm round her "Come on, Love, no time to cry, this should be a joyful moment" Dora encouraged as she drew her friend slowly towards the front door.

They were just going up the steps, and Higgs was getting the front door key out of his pocket when they heard a sound coming from the stable block.

"That sounded like a horse whinnying" said Higgs, "Do you think the Germans left the horses behind?"

"I certainly didn't see them in the convoy" Dora remembered.

"Wait there" Higgs warned the two women "I am going to investigate"

He left Dora and Maisie standing on the door step as he disappeared round the side of the house. He was gone some time and the pair sat down on the step to wait for his return.

"Do you think we should go and look for him" Maisie suggested.

"No. He will be alright" Dora reassured her "He told us to wait here and he will be annoyed if he thinks we have followed him"

After what seemed an age Higgs reappeared round the corner and there was someone else behind him in the shadows. As the two men came into the sunlight Maisie saw that it was Otto following Higgs.

"Otto!" she cried rushing forward. She ran to the boy and threw her arms around him. The two of them embraced and both were in tears as Higgs and Dora stood watching.

Higgs explained to his wife that he had found Otto crouching in the stables hiding behind the horses.

"When he saw me he looked terrified but when he realised who I was he calmed down and came out to meet me. He explained that the Germans were going to shoot the horses so he took them into the woods and hid them among the trees. He only came back to the stables when he was sure all the Germans had left" Higgs explained.

"But what will happen to him?" Dora protested "He has been left behind now. He cannot return to his regiment"

"No" Higgs agreed "This is going to be a huge problem"

"We can't give him up to become a prisoner of war" Maisie protested "We must hide him somehow"

Higgs looked doubtful. "I think that might be a criminal offence" he said

Dora, ever the practical one suggested that they might all go into the house and see if the kitchen was still functional. "We all deserve a nice cup of tea".

They went in and found that the German forces had left the kitchen in full working order. They had even left a full larder, so Dora was able to make them a nice lunch, and they all sat round the kitchen table discussing what they could do about the young fugitive who had come among them. "Quite like old times" Higgs laughed as he held his cup out for more tea.

When they had eaten the four of them began to explore the house. It was in surprisingly good condition.

"The Oberst would not tolerate any vandalism" Otto assured the others "He expected every one to respect the property. He regarded it as his home and he liked to live in luxury and comfort. Anybody who damaged anything was fined quite heavily,"

"Good thing too" Higgs agreed "He may have been a brute but at least he was a civilised brute"

Maisie went into her bedroom "Is this where the Oberst slept" she asked and Otto nodded.

"I will burn all the bedding" she announced emphatically "I am not going to sleep in anything that came anywhere near that revolting body"

The others laughed "You have got it in for him" Higgs chuckled.

"Indeed I have" Maisie replied "He and Hitler are definitely off my Christmas card list"

As the day wore on the problem of what to do about Oto became a pressing matter. It was Higgs who came up with a solution.

"WE must hide the boy here in the house" he suggested "There is plenty of room in that spacious attic. We can make a secure hideaway up there"

"Yes" agreed Maisie "Nobody is going to come and inspect the house, after all it is my home and all I have done is reclaim it."

"But it was an enemy Headquarters" Dora warned "maybe the British authorities will want to search for any incriminating evidence"

"If they do there will be nothing to find" Higgs told them "and they would not look up in the attic if we blocked off the entrance. We could pull a cupboard across the door to the stairway and any searchers would be unaware that there was another set of rooms up there. Otto could have access through the window onto the roof and could easily climb down to the window of the room below"

"Wouldn't that be dangerous?" Maisie feared.

"No I will show you" Higgs told her and they all went to inspect.

So it was agreed that Otto should remain in hiding at least until the war had ended. Maisie then intended to see if she could adopt him. He was still under twenty-one and could prove that he was an orphan as he had a letter officially informing him that both his parents had been killed in an air raid on Berlin.

"I hope the war ends while I am still officially a child" Otto said in a surprisingly deep, and adult voice.

Isle of Wight – Autumn 1945

With the end of the war the Islanders settled down again to normality. They would never forget the hardship of the years of occupation, but they were a resilient people, and they soon put the horrors behind them and began to enjoy their lovely island once again. But there were inevitable reminders.

The body of Mike Hardcastle was never found and it was believed that he had been buried in quicklime somewhere in the grounds of Parkhurst Prison. Harold mourned his friend and wanted to have some sort of memorial to him. He remembered the very courageous action Mike had taken in giving himself up to save the boys held captive in the grounds of Osborne House.

Harold set up a memorial fund which quickly amounted to a considerable sum. The islanders were grateful to the deceased spy. Harold commissioned a memorial stone that was laid by the roadside outside the prison. It was a simple slab engraved with the name *'Michael Hardcastle',* and the words *'In memory of a brave Englishman who came to the Isle of Wight to help the islanders during the German occupation.*

He gave his life to save young men held captive in the grounds of Osborne House. Grateful islanders salute him.

The stone was laid in a special ceremony attended by the many islanders who had benefited from Mike's courage and, to this day, there are always fresh flowers on the stone "Who puts them there? – we will never know.

Maisie went to London as soon as the war was over and pulled all the strings she could to make Otto her adopted son. She knew a lot of influential people and came back to the island triumphant. Having officially adopted Otto she set up ariding stables for him and he became very popular as an riding instructor. It is doubtful if any of his young pupils ever knew he was originally a German. He became a true English gentleman and was much respected on the island.

Maisie gave the lodge, together with a sizeable piece of land to Higgs, and he and Dora used it to run a successful market garden, supplying quality vegetables to greengrocers all over the island. Their son was demobbed but he never returned to the island, preferring to go into business on the mainland. He came to visit his parents infrequently, and the little bedroom that had been Maisie's home all through the occupation, was always kept ready for him.

Horace Brearley was killed in 1944 and his widow, Marika never returned to the island. After the war she returned to Germany where she lived in what was left of Berlin. She spent much of her time trying to get her elderly mother out of the Russian Sector. She never succeeded.

Fred Hopkins stayed on the Isle of Wight when he was released from Parkhurst Prison. He found his girl, Eileen, who had waited for him and they were married at St Thomas's Church in Newport early in 1946. Strangely enough he returned to Parkhurst Prison, but this time as a prison guard.

Endpiece

Isle of Wight - 1999

The old man sat by the fire reading his paper. His wife was in the kitchen baking a cake for his birthday the following day. He put his paper down and stared into the fire "Seventy years old tomorrow" he thought, "Three score years and ten. What a life I have had, so full of ups and downs". His thoughts were disturbed by the sound of the garden gate closing. He looked out of the window and saw a young woman coming down the path towards the cottage. She knocked on the door.

"Get that will you, Love" his wife called from the kitchen "My hands are covered in flour"

"I'm on my way" he replied. He opened the door and just for a moment he thought his eyes were deceiving him "Issy?" he questioned.

"No, not Issy" replied the young woman standing on the doorstep "I am her Granddaughter. You must be my Great Uncle Jack"

Jack stared at the young woman, he seemed rooted to the spot.

"Aren't you going to ask our visitor to come in" said Jack's wife, Martha, coming up behind him, wiping her hands on her apron.

Jack stood aside to let the woman enter.

"Come in , Dear" greeted Martha "You must excuse Jack, he seems to be in a state of shock"

"I am so sorry" laughed their visitor "I did not mean to startle him, my name is Heidi and I am his sister's Granddaughter"

Jack recovered himself and stood aside while Martha ushered Heidi into the sitting room and took her coat from her.

"Come and sit by the fire and get warm while I make some tea." . said Martha.

Jack stared at Heidi, she looked so like Issy. She was tall and slim with blonde hair tied back in a ponytail.

She had the same bright blue eyes as Issy and a dimple in her right cheek when she smiled.

"Please forgive me" jack splutterd, "You look so like my sister, I thought for a moment that she had come back. But, of course, she would not look like you now, she will be an old lady"

"She would have been seventy seven but, sadly, she died three years ago." Heidi told the old man.

"Oh dear" he replied "I wish I could have seen her again. You say she was your Grandmother so you must have known her well. Please tell me about her"

"Yes, we were good friends. We spent much time together. My Mother, Maria, is her eldest daughter and I have a photo for you. It is of four generations" Heidi dived into her capacious handbag and produced a photograph. She leaned over and gave it to Jack.

"There is Issy" she said pointing to an elegant, elderly lady wearing a smart summer dress, her grey hair piled on her head, held by a large, tortoiseshell pin "and there is my Mother sitting next to her holding my daughter Berthe. I am standing behind them" she continued.

Jack looked at the picture and tears came to his eyes.

"She looks lovely" he whispered "in fact you all look lovely. What a wonderful family. How old is your child?"

"Berthe is five years old now. That picture was taken just before her first birthday" she informed the old man.

"How many children did Issy have?" Jack wanted to know.

"She had two sons and two daughters" Heidi told him. "My Mother, Maria was the first, then came my Uncle Jack. He was named for you" she paused as the old man took a handkerchief from his pocket and noisily blew his nose.

"Then came my Uncle Wolf, and the youngest was my Aunt Angela." She continued.

"All those children, and I never knew" Jack moaned. "Why did she never get in touch? Why did she never come home?"

"I think she felt guilty for leaving. She often spoke of you and your parents, but she felt she could not come back. She and my Grandfather travelled a lot but they never came to Britain" the young woman told Jack.

Martha came in with a tray of tea and biscuits. She asked Heidi what had brought her to the Isle of Wight. Heidi sipped her tea before explaining.

"I am a doctor" she told them "I have been in London attending a medical conference. I thought I would take a few days holiday when the meetings were over, and I have always wanted to see my Grandmother's childhood home, so I decided to take a trip to the island".

"Well, you are very welcome" Martha cooed, "Jack has always wondered what happened to his sister"

"Issy married Franz as soon the war ended. They lived in Bonn where Grandfather practiced as a lawyer. All their children were born there. My Mother and my

Uncle Wolf became lawyers like Grandfather, Uncle Jack is in banking and Aunt Angela is a nurse. Wolf is married and has two sons, Jack is a bachelor and Angela is married but has no children. I have one brother called Franz after Grandfather and he is also a doctor. He is engaged to be married to a Dutch girl. I am married to a doctor and we now live in Berlin. Berthe was born there. Issy often came to stay with us after Franz died. So that is our family" she finished.

There was a silence while Jack digested all the information. At last he spoke, "Well, I am so pleased to hear that all went well with Issy" he said at last.

Heidi nodded "Yes" she agreed "Grandmama had a good life. I think her only regret was that she could not share it with you. Actually she knew all about you because a friend of hers visited the Isle of Wight some years ago and did a bit of research for her"

"Oh!" exclaimed Jack "I wish I had known. But it's too late to worry about that now"

Heidi stood up "I must be off" she said "I am booked on the 2.30 car ferry. Thank you for the tea"

As she bent to kiss Jack on both cheeks she handed him an envelope "Here are some more photos for you, also my address so you can keep in touch with the family. It was so good to meet you after all these years. I hope to see you again"

She kissed Martha and thanked her again for her hospitality and then she was gone.

Jack watched her climb into her car and drive off "Goodbye Issy" he whispered as the car disappeared round the bend.

The End

(Of course, none of this ever happened – but it might well have done)

About the author:

Anne Crofton Dearle came to the Isle of Wight when she was three weeks old and lived in Freshwater Bay until just before her third birthday. She returned to the island to live in Cowes with her husband in the summer of 2013.

Anne took up writing when she retired from teaching and is the author of a series of children's books featuring the twins Zack & Zoe, and she has also written a futuristic story called "The Summer of 3012". Her book introducing William Shakespeare to children ("The Treasure Trail") has been adopted as a text book by several schools on the mainland. This was followed by an adult version called "A Cottage in Shottery"

Read the beginning of Anne Crofton Dearle's novella, "A Cottage in Shottery". It is the story of two women who played an important part in the life of William Shakespeare – his wife, Anne, and his younger daughter, Judith.

"A Cottage in Shottery" is available in paperback and as an e-book from Amazon.co.uk. and can be found by entering Anne Crofton Dearle's page on their website.

A Cottage in Shottery.

My Story - by Anne

I remember the first time I lay with Will. It was a lovely, warm August evening and we had walked across the fields until we came to a stream. We kicked off our shoes and splashed our feet in the cool water. He put his arm round me, and as I turned to watch a kingfisher flying over the water he pulled me towards him and kissed my lips, tenderly at first and then with passion. Before I knew it we were making love there on the grass by the stream.

Will was only a boy, just eighteen years old, but to me he was a man. He was so good looking with his dark curly hair and twinkling eyes. He was tall and muscular, and when he walked there was a spring in his step, almost as if he wanted to dance. He was clever too, always ready with a witty remark. He was so warm and affectionate and he made me forget that I was his senior by eight years. He made me feel like a young girl rather than a spinster racing past marriageable age.

After that first time we met often and walked out into the country to find a secluded spot to make love. I fell in love with Will that summer and thought he loved me too. I was very vulnerable at that time as it was just coming up to the first anniversary of my father's death. My mother had been dead since I was a child, and my brother had moved away to run his own farm when he married. So my father was my closest companion. Will filled that gap in my life and made me happy for the first time in months.

I had known Will slightly for years. I used to see him in Stratford when I went to market with my father. I would see him running between the stalls with his brother, and I once watched him steal an apple. He saw me watching and winked at me as he put his finger to his lips swearing me to secrecy. I remember laughing and nodding as an agreement not to tell.

I never knew him to speak to until early August 1582 when I went again to the market, this time with my brother. As I went to buy fruit I slipped on a ripe plum that someone had dropped on the ground. I would have fallen had Will not been standing right behind me. He caught me in his arms and I felt the warmth of his body as he lifted me up. I regained my balance and turned to thank him. He smiled and said "You must be shaken by your near fall, come and have a jug of ale with me to settle your nerves"

I looked around for my brother but he was nowhere in sight so I agreed to go to the inn. "I think I know you" I said to my rescuer "Are you not Will Shakespeare?"

"And I would like to know you" he replied "so tell me your name, pretty wench".

"I am Anne Hathaway" I told him "and I come from Shottery"

We sat side by side and sipped our ale. We chatted like old friends and time slipped by unnoticed until suddenly the inn door slammed open and there was my brother, Bartholomew, standing with hands on hips, his face angrily glowering at me.

"I have been looking everywhere for you, Sister" he shouted "What are you doing sitting in this inn with a stranger? Have you no shame?"

I was angry to be so accused "Stop shouting at me" I stormed "this gentleman saved me from falling and he offered me a drink to steady my nerves after the shock. If you were half a man you would have been on hand to help me when I tripped. What sort of a brother do you think you are, you miserable specimen of a man"

Bartholomew calmed down and looked rather shamefaced.

Will invited Bartholomew to join us for a drink "My name is Will Shakespeare" he announced "and I would be friends" Reluctantly my brother shook Will's hand and he even decided to go and buy more drinks for the three of us. While he was away Will whispered in my ear "I like your spirit, young Anne. You stood up to your brother and I admired that"

That was when he asked me to walk out with him and, of course, I agreed.

After that Will would walk over to Shottery to meet me whenever he could. He told me he was apprenticed to a lawyer in Stratford and he had to work long hours preparing documents for his Master.

He usually had time off after church on Sunday, but he did not come every week. I would stand at the farm gate each Sunday hoping he would come, and was often downhearted when he did not appear, but the times he did come made up for the disappointment.

Towards the end of September, as the evenings were drawing in, Will came to Shottery less often. He said that his Master was busy and needed him, so he had less free time. He promised to come to me when he could, and I believed him. I think I was blinded by love.

In October he came only once to Shottery. He made the excuse that we could not go walking in the evening now it was dark so early. I said that he could come and spend an evening with me at the farm, and that my brother and his wife would like to invite him for supper. I did not notice that he failed to reply because he pulled me into the shadow of a tree and began kissing me passionately. Of course I responded and all else was forgotten.

At the end of October I missed my monthly courses for a second time and realised that I was with child. I needed to tell Will but he did not come again, and I was frantic. My sister-in-law, Martha, noticed that I was fretful and was not eating my food. She asked me what was troubling me and I burst into tears. I confessed my condition and she put her arms round me and held me as I wept.

It was thus that my brother found us when he came home from the fields. "What ails you, Sister, that you need comforting?" he asked.

Martha told him that I was with child and he looked stunned. "Who is the father?" he wanted to know. "He must marry you before you give birth"

I did not want to tell, but Martha knew that I had been seeing Will and she guessed he was to blame "Is it Will Shakespeare?" she asked me and I nodded.

My brother exploded "He will marry you or I will kill him" he vowed.

Martha intervened "Do not be so foolish" she admonished "the boy will not be much use to Anne if he is dead. No more talk of killing if you please. Anne must tell Will of her plight and appeal to his better nature"

■ ■

Read 'A Cottage in Shottery' to find out what happened in Anne's story, and then go on to find out her daughter, Judith's version of events. Available in both paperback and as an e-book from Amazon.co.uk

11807072R00115

Printed in Great Britain
by Amazon.co.uk, Ltd.,
Marston Gate.